JUN 1 6 2014

CHRIS D'LACEY

UNICORNE FILES

BOOK ONE

A DARK INHERITANCE

SCHOLASTIC PRESS

NEW YORK

Library of Congress Cataloging-in-Publication Data

d'Lacey, Chris, author.
A dark inheritance / Chris d'Lacey. — First edition.
pages cm. — (UNICORNE files ; book one)
Summary: When Michael Malone saves a dog, he discovers that he
has paranormal abilities, which bring him to the attention of a secret
organization, UNICORNE — but he plans to use the ability to find
out what happened to his father, who mysteriously vanished three years
earlier, and save his new friend, Freya.
ISBN 978-0-545-60876-3 (jacketed hardcover) 1. Missing persons —
Juvenile fiction. 2. Secret societies — Juvenile fiction. 3. Mothers and
sons — Juvenile fiction. 4. Friendship — Juvenile fiction. 5. Paranormal
fiction. 6. Adventure stories. [1. Mystery and detective stories.
2. Missing persons — Fiction. 3. Secret societies — Fiction. 4. Mothers
and sons — Fiction. 5. Friendship — Fiction. 6. Supernatural — Fiction
7. Adventure and adventurers — Fiction.] I. Title.
PZ7.D6475Db 2014
813.6 — dc23
2013027397

10 9 8 7 6 5 4 3 2 1   14 15 16 17 18

Printed in the U.S.A.   23

First edition, June 2014

The text type was set in Caslon.

The display type was set in Bank Gothic.

Book design by Christopher Stengel

TABLE OF CONTENTS

It was the day Mom took the coast road to school.

The day I tried to save a suicidal husky.

One day before I would begin to wonder if my father was still alive.

"Mom, *why* are we going this way?" moaned Josie.

The car had hit a pothole and bounced my sister up from her video game console. She rubbed her window with the side of her fist and saw the wide green spaces of Berry Head. Beyond it, just a few hundred yards to her right, lay the cliffs and the spiraling drop to the sea.

I already knew how Mom was going to answer. I'd heard the radio broadcast at breakfast. A burst water main on the outskirts of Holton Byford. It didn't take a genius to know there would be holdups on our normal route to school.

"Flooding," Mom muttered, crunching the gears. The Range Rover lurched and slowed a little. Mom hit the gear-shift again, forcing the car into third. She was a pretty good driver, but she'd never come to grips with a manual shift.

"Flooding?" Josie wrinkled her nose. She questioned

nearly everything Mom came out with. It got them into arguments. But not today.

The car slowed again, then rolled to a stop.

Mom sighed like a tire deflating. Best-laid plans. I could read it on her lips.

"What's the matter?" I asked, closing my book. I was halfway through a chapter of *The Illustrated Man*.

"Police," she said.

"Cool." Josie craned her neck sideways to see. She liked the police and wanted to join them when she was older. She had a mind for criminal detection, she said. She was smart, my sister, there was no denying that. She was into sudoku and crosswords and stuff. But it didn't make her Sherlock Holmes. Not yet.

I could see the cars now through the slanting drizzle, two of them angled in to block the road, their roof lights circling like bright blue whips. We had the wheels to go around them, over the grass. But Mom wasn't the type to run against the law. She fussed with a curl of her hair and waited.

A patrolman wearing a lemon-colored jacket walked toward us, making window signals. Mom hit a button. Her window slid down. The salt tangs of the rainwashed sea swept in, bringing the cold of early spring with it.

The policeman took off his hat. Despite the rain, there was sweat on his brow.

"I'm sorry, you'll have to turn back," he said. He had a thin face full of shades and angles, the dark shadow of his close-shaved cheeks echoing the raven-black crop of his hair.

"Why?" said Josie, hitting him at once with the full indignation that only a ten-year-old could muster.

He didn't even look at her. He said to Mom, "There's been an incident."

"A jumper?" my sister gasped.

"*Jo-sie!*" Mom winced apologetically and covered the flush of blood to her neck.

The policeman put on his hat, adjusting it once with a tug of the peak. The Berry Head cliff was famous for suicides. We all knew that. Even Sherlock.

"If you'd turn the vehicle around, please, and head back into Holton."

"Seriously?" said Mom. She studied the way ahead. Beyond the cars, there was nothing to see. A tilted signpost was the only hint of drama.

The policeman nodded. "The road will be closed for an hour at least."

Mom's shoulders slumped. But before her hand could reach for reverse, Josie came to the rescue. Stroking her ponytail against her shoulder, she said, "Oh, but I'll be late for school, *Officer.*"

Officer. That was cute. She knew how to play people,

Josie Malone. Despite her youth, she already had a fan club of male admirers. Valentine's Day was a serious time for cardboard recycling at our house.

The "officer" straightened his muscular shoulders. His yellow jacket crackled. He stroked his chin. He seemed to like the attention this kid was giving him, liked that she was showing some degree of respect. He made a weak attempt to stand his ground.

"I'm sorry for the inconvenience, but —"

"I've got my music test at nine. My finals — for flute."

Flute? I threw Josie a sideways glance. Mom, to her credit, didn't even flinch. Josie couldn't carry a tune in a bucket. She could barely blow a whistle, never mind a flute. But, boy, she had a major talent for stories.

She thickened the plot.

"It's for my scholarship. I've been rehearsing my Mozart every night for *months*, haven't I, Mom?"

"She's . . . very dedicated," Mom chipped in, looking as if she'd like to ooze into the floorboard.

The policeman looked uneasy. Now he had a disaffected parent and a dewy-eyed little girl testing his resolve. He bit his lip and looked back at the patrol cars.

"What exactly has happened?" asked Mom, in the kind of voice that would have made the devil confess his sins.

A second went by. The windshield wipers beat their rhythm, the metronome of everyone's ticking heart.

The engine's cooling fan came on.

Josie put her console aside.

"A walker reported a dog," said the cop.

Mom shrugged. "Lots of people walk their dogs here."

"Well, that's just it." The policeman stubbed his boot on the ground. "The dog is running at the edge of the cliff — but we can't find any sign of an owner."

"Maybe it's a stray?" Mom suggested, avoiding the thought stacking up in our minds.

The policeman shook his head. "It's a breed — with a collar. You don't get many strays like that, not wandering around up here, anyway."

"Okay," Josie said, "here's how it is." She cracked her knuckles in the dip of her lap. She was now the investigating officer. "Catch the dog and check its name tag. It's bound to have a name tag and an address. You can call the address to see if the owner is missing. If you find the owner, that means they haven't jumped. Then you'll know that the dog has just run away — or maybe been stolen and dumped here, yeah?"

There was a pause while everyone considered their verdict. Eventually, the policeman said to Mom, "Bright spark, isn't she? High IQ?"

"Off the scale," said Mom. "Not a musical one."

He rested his forearm against the car and gradually slanted his gaze toward Josie. "Yes, miss, we've thought of all that. The problem is —"

"You can't catch the dog," I muttered. Though they'd tried. Hence the sweat on the cop's brow.

"Correct," he said. "It's . . . resisting arrest." He pulled his mouth into a half-crooked smile. "And now it's too close to the drop for comfort. Are you all right, son? You look a bit peaky."

"He has asthma," said Josie, hearing me wheeze.

But that wasn't strictly true. Lately, I'd been having these peculiar moments when my breathing faltered and my head would go light. The doctors were calling it a type of asthma, because they couldn't find another explanation for it. The "attacks," when they came, always followed a pattern: a fierce tightness in the chest, a slight blurring of vision. A few puffs on my inhaler would usually put me right. But on the last two occasions, things had been different. The symptoms had sped up and been more pronounced. I'd had this weird sensation of floating, as though my mind wasn't quite in sync with my body. I hadn't dared tell Mom or the doctors about it — I was scared they'd think I was crazy. Deep down, I'd been hoping it would just go away.

I could see the dog on the headland now. A gray-and-white husky running back and forth like a distressed wolf.

The rain thumped hard against Josie's window.

A powerful gust of wind billowed like an air bag inside the car.

And the longer I looked at that troubled dog, the closer I seemed to get to its thoughts.

"It's going to jump," I breathed.

"What?" said Josie. She was patting my pockets for my inhaler.

I heard the policeman saying, "Look, as you're the only vehicle here, I'll see what I can do. If we wave you through, you drive on normally, agreed?"

"Thank you," said Mom.

"It's gonna jump," I said again.

And I opened my door.

I hardly felt the rain as I started to run. I vaguely heard the policeman shouting, "Hey, come back! What are you doing?" Then the tightness in my chest reached fever pitch and my visual senses just seemed to explode. The grass and the rain blurred into a smear and I was moving faster than I'd ever thought possible. In an instant, I was at the edge of the cliff where the soil likes to crumble and the distant water wants to pull you down. Through a tunnel of vision, I saw the drop. A deep gray maw of angry waves and jagged rocks. The dog was on its haunches, ready to spring. There was rain in its eyes, mist in its fur, torment in its thumping husky heart.

For a nanosecond, I seemed to just hover — a helpless observer, studying life in a microdot of time. Then through the rush of noise came a calmness. And the next thing I knew, I was on the ground with the dog howling and wriggling in my arms. The wind was ripping at the gaps in my clothing, cursing me for stealing its prize. The earth around my head began to pound like the skin of a wet bass drum. Shadows fell across me, blocking the rain. Black boots landed like cannon shots. Then it was a muddle of hands and voices and crackling jackets and slithering dampness and frantic barking. One policeman took the dog by the collar. A panicked voice cried, "It's all right, I've got him." I wasn't sure if they meant me or the dog, but the animal was yanked away from my grip, and my arms were clamped and they dragged me to safety.

I was barely on my feet when Mom slammed into me. "Oh my God, Michael, what were you *thinking*?" She put her hands to my face so I couldn't look away. "I was so frightened. You could have been *killed*!"

I glanced back at our car and saw Josie in the rain underneath an umbrella. She was taking pictures with her cell phone.

The original policeman was kneeling beside us. He was gasping for breath, staring blankly at the ground. A raindrop fattened his veiny cheek. He wiped a little drool off his bottom lip. "How did that happen?" he panted. "One moment you were right by the car, then . . ." He turned and squinted at the fuzzy horizon. "How could that possibly *happen*?"

By now, the cold was creeping under my clothing. Shivering, I said to Mom, "Where's the dog?"

"In the van," said the officer who was marshaling me.

"Michael, forget about the dog," Mom snapped. She sounded weary, ready to break.

I met her worried gaze. "It was going to jump."

She shook her head as if to say, *What are you talking about?*

But I couldn't explain it, not to her, not to anyone. Somehow, I'd moved from the car to the cliff as if I'd passed through an invisible teleport.

"Oh, that's all we want." The policeman holding me passed me to Mom and went to head off a couple of new arrivals. A woman in a beige-colored, high-collared raincoat, and a man toting a chunky camera. Journalists, by the look of them.

"Come on, I'm taking you home." Mom turned me away, pausing to say a brief thank-you to the policeman still on the ground.

"We may need to speak to you again," he called.

But Mom wasn't stopping. She bundled me past the inquisitive journalists and ordered Josie to get into the car.

As I strapped on my seat belt, the woman in the raincoat appeared at Mom's window. "Hi, Candy Streetham from the *Holton Post*." She held up an ID card. "Do you want to tell me what just happened here? Your son's been a bit of a hero, hasn't he?"

"I'm sorry, they're very late for school," Mom said. She put the Rover into gear and drove away, grinding up a section of Berry Head turf.

Candy Streetham and her upturned collar disappeared behind a moving sheet of glass.

As we found the road again and bumped our way down it, something fell off the seat beside me. I reached down and picked up a small black case. "What's this?"

Josie tutted and snatched it off me. "Luckily for you, I won't be needing that today. I can take my test next week instead."

"Test?"

She frowned and put the case into her bag. "Flute, stupid."

And she picked up her console and started a new game.

2 · WEIRDO

Mom took us home first and made me undress in the center of the kitchen. My uniform was streaked with grass stains and mud. Everything except my blue-spotted boxer shorts went into the washing machine, including my socks. Some hero I looked. Josie took a picture and labeled it LADYKILLER. She would dine out on this for weeks.

After showering, I put on my spare school stuff and came downstairs and sat in the living room.

Mom called from the kitchen, "Don't get too complacent, you pair. You're going to school as soon as I'm done."

"Whatever," Josie sighed, and continued texting. Which reminded me — her phone. She had photos of me and the dog on her phone.

But as I leaned forward to speak to her, the doorbell gave a lengthy ring.

"Would one of you get that, please?"

I glanced through the front window. "Mom, it's that reporter again."

"*What?*" Mom sounded like a wasp in a bottle.

"The woman at Berry Head."

"And the man," Josie added, jumping up to take a look.

Mom came through, drying her hands on a towel. "I don't believe it. Have they actually followed us home?" She checked the window and headed for the hall. "Stay there, you two."

Yeah. As if.

We peered into the hall as Mom opened the door to Candy Streetham.

"Hi," said the raincoat girl, flashing a smile any toothpaste manufacturer would have been proud of.

Dazzled, Mom found herself a little off guard. "Look —"

Ms. Streetham instantly filled the gap. "It's okay, we don't want to keep you. We got most of what we needed from the boys in blue. Quite a drama. Sorry we missed it. Just wondered if we might have a quote from Michael?" She flipped me a wave. "It is Michael, isn't it?"

Even if she'd wanted to, Mom had no time to register her hurt. Our names were common knowledge to members of the press. Any seasoned reporter in Holton Byford was aware that this ivy-strewn, eighteenth-century cottage was home to the tragic Malone family. Just over three years ago, my dad had walked out of the house to catch a business flight to New

Mexico. He had never come back. It was the hole in our life that we tried not to talk about. His disappearance had made the national news.

Barely pausing for breath, Candy went on, "Brave boy, your son. Why'd you do it, Michael? What was going through your mind when you got out of the car?"

"He thought the dog was going to jump," said Josie.

"Josie, be quiet," Mom said curtly.

But there was no stopping Candy Streetham now. "Didn't I see you flashing a cell phone?"

I felt Josie nod.

"Pictures or movie?"

My heart thumped. Josie's camera was state-of-the-art. Had she managed to film me ghosting on disk?

No was the answer. "Pictures," she said.

Candy aimed a pistol-shaped hand at her. "That's my girl. Do you want to show Eddie?"

The cameraman smiled. He had swept-back hair almost down to his shoulders and pitted skin around his lightly tanned cheeks. He had a stud in one ear and a scar along his neck. His eyes were the color of a pebble beach.

"Look, they should have been at school half an hour ago," Mom said, stepping sideways to block an approach. "And I am also late for work."

And I've only got one pair of hands, Josie mouthed, mimicking the usual follow-up line. Since Mom had gone back to full-time work, she'd been talking, on and off, about hiring an au pair.

"Seriously, this won't take long," said Candy. "It would be awesome for us to have a picture of Michael with the dog."

Josie was already thumbing her folders. "Will it be in the paper tonight?"

"Front page," said Eddie, checking his lens.

"We don't want that sort of exposure," said Mom. She crossed her arms. Always a bad sign.

Candy changed her approach. "Trust me, I do understand." She tucked a sickle-shaped frond of hair behind her ear. Despite the breadth of her tooth-whitened smile, her attempt at sympathy had all the sincerity of a James Bond villain. The wind whipped sideways across the step. She rubbed one foot against the back of her calf. "After everything you've been through —"

"Still going through."

"— more press is the last thing you need. But the story's going to be splashed all over the papers, anyway. Bravery in kids is headline stuff. People will want to put a face to the name. If I owned the dog, I'd want to know who'd saved it from those rocks."

"Who is the owner?" I asked as Josie handed over her phone.

Candy ignored me and paged through the pictures. She touched one and fed the phone back to Eddie, asking him quietly what he thought. "Too distant," he said, with a shake of his head.

A black cloud formed over Josie's space.

"Though I'd like to take this one back to the office." He spread his fingers to enlarge a pic.

"Really?" said Candy. "Bit blurred, isn't it?"

"I might be able to work with it," he said. "It's amazing what you can get from a digital shot." He glanced at me again as he flipped out the memory card.

Before any of us could object, he'd fed the card into a slot on his camera and was busily uploading Josie's images.

Meanwhile, Candy turned to Mom again. "Could we have a picture of Michael, anyway? Just as a backup. Out here, maybe?" She grinned like a weather girl predicting sunny spells.

Mom's chest expanded with air.

"I don't mind, Mom." I just wanted to be done with it now so I could go to school and forget about the cliff. I was missing English, my favorite subject. I touched Mom's arm and stepped out of the house.

They arranged me on the lawn, but away from the cedar tree, wanting the meadow in the background, they said. Eddie asked me to raise my hands level with my chest, as if to say, *Hey, it was nothing. I save dogs all the time.* He took shots of me smiling and a few more of me looking concerned. The camera seemed to click about fifty times before he was satisfied he'd got what he wanted.

"All done. Camera loves you," Candy said. She reached up and tousled my hair.

"My mom's waiting," I muttered, and tried to push past, but Candy stopped me and drew me so close I could see the faults in her peach-colored makeup.

"Why did you think the dog was going to jump?"

"Don't know."

"But you sensed it, right?" Suddenly, her tone had changed, as if she'd sharpened her tongue on the bare edge of truth.

"I don't know," I said again. "I've got to go."

"What about the cliff?" She stepped across me slightly. "The dog was half a soccer field from the road. How did you get to the edge so fast?"

I glanced at Eddie, who was watching me keenly. "I'm good at running."

"Really?" She pulled her eyebrows tight. "You don't strike me as a sprinter, Michael. Tall, a little skinny, more marathon man than Usain Bolt." She picked a piece of random fluff off my jacket. "Let me tell you the thing I'm struggling with here: None of the cops remembers seeing you catch the dog. Do you want to comment on that?"

"Excuse me, are you done there?" Mom had my school bag in hand and was locking up the house.

"Almost!" Candy turned to me again. "They're saying it was like something superhuman took over. Like a force they didn't understand rushed in." She tilted her head. Her hair fell down as straight as harp strings.

Eddie swung his camera to the opposite hand.

"It was misty," I said, and this time I got away from her. Candy sighed and clicked her tongue in frustration. But how could I possibly describe what had happened when I didn't even understand it myself?

"Right," said Mom as I reached the porch step, "no more shenanigans." For the second time that morning, she bundled us into the car.

At the end of the driveway, we had to pause for traffic. Candy was walking back to her car, swinging her hips like Holton Byford's next top model. Despite the tension of the last few moments, there was still one thing I needed to know. Lowering the window, I asked her again, "Did you find out who owns the dog?"

She put her hands into her pockets and shivered. She tumbled my question around on her tongue before deciding she would give me an answer. "The dog's called Trace and it seems to belong to —"

"Candy, let's go," Eddie called over. He was leaning on the open door of their car.

"Yeah, one moment."

"The office wants us. Now."

"Chill out," Candy said to him. "What's the rush?" She fished out a notebook. "The girl's name is Freya Zielinski."

"Freya?" I almost spat the name back.

I thought I saw Eddie frown.

Candy's pencil-thin eyebrows twitched. "You know her?"

Of course. Everyone knew *Freya*. She was in my class. The weirdo in the corner who everyone ignored. "Is she dead?" I asked. I didn't like the girl much. None of us did. Even so, it made me sick to think of her jumping.

Again, Candy didn't try to answer quickly. But before she could offer any sort of reply, Mom had gunned the throttle and we were on our way.

"Who's Freya?" Josie asked as we sped toward Holton.

I caught Mom's eyes in the rearview mirror. "No one," I muttered, looking away.

"She must be *someone* or you wouldn't have recognized her name."

"She's a new girl at school."

"The one who looks like she lives in a coffin?"

A common description of Freya, yes. Vamp was a name they taunted her with. Or Crow. In the eyes of the popular crowd, Freya's dress sense was lifted right out of a scarecrow manual.

"I've seen her around," Josie babbled on. "Mad hair, like it's been cut with a hedge trimmer. Massive sleep bags under her eyes. Slums about in a hoodie. It was *her* dog?"

"Josie, just shut up, okay?"

"Only asking." She stuck out her tongue.

"All right, you two." Mom had heard enough. She put the radio on to break up the argument.

"She's no one," I said to my reflection in the glass.

The pale-skinned goth who sketched pictures of dragons. The freak who'd left behind an orphan dog. Freya Zielinski, victim of a horrible bone-crushing death.

She was no one.

No one at all.

I finally got to school around ten fifteen. I slipped into the classroom as quietly as I could. Mr. Hambleton was reading what sounded like a poem. Something to do with the sea, bizarrely. He raised his voice to quash the swell of catcalls that greeted my entrance and gestured to my seat without pausing to ask for an explanation. I looked over my shoulder at Freya's desk.

Empty.

I felt sick.

"Thought she'd got you." I glanced sideways at the class clown, Ryan Garvey. He pulled his collar away from his neck and placed two fingers where the bite holes ought to go. That piece of pantomime somehow escaped Mr. Hambleton's attention, but the tongue-lolling death rasp that followed it didn't.

"Thank you, Ryan."

Garvey snapped to attention. "What for, sir?"

"For volunteering to explain the metaphorical significance of that final stanza."

"That what?"

The class erupted with laughter.

Mr. Hambleton walked down the room and placed the open book on Ryan's desk. "Forgive me. I seem to have mistaken your display for an artistic interpretation of the hungry sea. Clearly, I was wrong. So perhaps you'd like to copy the poem out in full and present me with your real thoughts during recess." He tapped the page.

"*Sir?*"

"That's not an invitation, that's an order, Ryan. Mr. Malone," he said, turning to me. "How good of you to join us. I take it there's a reason for your delayed engagement?"

I explained about the flooding.

"Well, I got here on time," Lauren Shenton said. She lived on the next road over from me.

Mr. Hambleton's face said she'd made a fair point. Several kids had come through the center of Holton, where the main had burst.

"We took the coast road," I said, fidgeting a little. "We were stopped by the police."

"How exciting," Mr. Hambleton said, raising his hand to quell the tide of comments. "I never had you down as a villain, Michael. Nothing serious, I hope?"

I shrugged. They would find out soon enough.

"Well, you're here, that's all that matters. Right —"

"Sir?"

He was about to go striding back to the front. "Yes, Michael?"

"Where's Freya?"

"Avoiding sunlight," someone muttered.

Mr. Hambleton let the taunt pass. "I believe Freya called in this morning to say she was taking care of her father, who's been ill."

"Bet she's staked him," someone else said. And even though the logic didn't really add up, the class collapsed in laughter again.

"That's enough!" Mr. Hambleton had reached his limit. He glared at the bigmouths and troublemakers. "I have it on good authority that Freya went through a difficult, life-threatening operation when she was younger. She came to Holton with her father to make a new start. If I hear one more slur about vampires or crows or staking of hearts, I will make *all* of you read Bram Stoker's *Dracula* and then require an essay from each of you on the moral agenda that underpins the general story arc. Is that clear?"

"Yes, sir," we said, like terrified rabbits.

Lauren Shenton flapped a hand in the air.

"Yes, Lauren, what now?"

"Sir, no one really wants to dis Freya, but, you know, she

won't get involved. It's like she doesn't *want* to make friends with us. Like she's scared of people or something."

"Then you must be patient and give her time."

"And she talks to herself," someone said.

"She's freaky. Her face is weird," Ryan muttered.

"You should talk," Lauren said.

"No, it is, though," Ryan countered. "She kind of . . . changes. Don't you think?"

Several kids nodded and someone else said, "And she's *always* drawing stupid dragons. That's like something you do when you're *nine*."

In the whirl of Mr. Hambleton's exasperation, I managed to inject a meaningful question. "Sir, what operation did Freya have?"

The other kids looked at me as if I'd defected to a foreign power. Why the sudden interest in Freya Zielinski?

Mr. Hambleton took a moment to think. "I'm not sure I'm at liberty to discuss that, Michael. Right, let's get on. Notebooks open, please."

I swung my school bag onto my desk, giving Ryan enough cover to pass me a note: *Blood transfusion*, it said.

What? I mouthed.

Freya's operation, he mouthed right back.

I wadded up the paper and threw it at his big, dense skull.

Somewhere up the road, I swear there's a village missing its idiot.

The rest of that day passed by without incident. Although my thoughts were still jumbled by the morning's events, school went on as normal around me, and no announcement came about Freya. Maybe she hadn't been at Berry Head at all and someone else had been walking her dog? But as far as I knew, Freya lived alone with her father — who was sick. So what was the husky doing up there?

And something else didn't compute. Later that day, I was passing the gym, when I looked in and saw Josie behind a music stand, practicing the flute. I watched for a minute, impressed by the way she moved her head to the flight of the music without ever shifting her gaze from the score. Eventually, Mrs. McNiece, her music teacher, opened the door a crack and asked if I needed to speak to my sister. I shook my head but asked, "Ma'am, is Josie good — at flute?"

She looked at me as if I'd swapped my brain for a sock. "Yes, of course she is. She's a wonderful prospect. She's at the level of a child much older than her years. But surely you knew that already?"

I nodded and got around it by saying that me and Mom just wanted to know how likely it was that Josie would get through her exam next week.

"Well, I'm not a betting person, but I'd say she's a certainty. Are you all right, Michael? You look as if the world's just folded in around you."

Pretty good description. Maybe it had.

"I'm fine, ma'am," I said, retreating into a stream of passing kids. I waved at Josie, who saw me and frowned but didn't stop playing.

Mrs. McNiece sighed and closed the door.

And that was that. Josie played the flute and played it well. And with every note that followed me down the corridor, the more my mind began to accept it. Until, by the end of school that day, I was certain I'd known it all along. Josie had played since she was six years old. She had an ear for music. A precocious talent.

Why was I even asking the question?

The following morning, outside the school gates, everything I knew about my life began to change. Within moments of being dropped off by Mom, the heckling began.

"Hey, Flash, show us your laser-powered feet!"

"Did they send you for a DOPE test afterward or what?"

"Why didn't you keep going, right over the cliff, and make an even bigger SPLASH, eh, hero?"

"What are they going on about?" Josie tutted as kids began to crowd around and jostle us.

Suddenly, Ryan burst to the front of the mob, thrusting a rolled-up notebook in my face, like it was a TV reporter's microphone. "Mr. Malone. Ryan Garvey, BBC News. Have you anything more to tell us about your dramatic cliff-top rescue —"

"*Thrilling* cliff-top rescue. Get it right," someone said.

Then I saw the newspaper.

Josie snatched it out of Freddie Hancock's hands.

"Michael, look," she said, passing the paper to me. "There's a picture and everything."

Underneath a headline that said HEROIC BOY RESCUES DOG was a picture of me standing on Berry Head with a husky in my arms.

"No . . . it didn't happen like that," I said.

Ryan Garvey aimed his "microphone" again. "How *did* it happen, Michael? What was going through your mind when you grabbed the dog? Was it anything to do with how many cans of dog food you'd get as a reward?"

Laughter.

I thrust the paper back at them and knocked Ryan's notebook out of my face. "The picture's a fake." Now I knew why Eddie had made me pose with my arms held out. It would have been a simple matter to paste a picture of the dog across my chest, then superimpose it on an image of rain-swept Berry Head. I wasn't even sure it was the same dog. And if that had been his intent all along, why had he bothered to take the images from Josie's phone?

"This is boring. I'm going in," said Josie. She skipped away to be with her friends.

Meanwhile, the mob was still giving me grief. There were more dumb jokes about bionic limbs and sled dog teams ("When's your next polar expedition, Michael?"). Then Ryan said something that stopped me in my tracks. "Where did you hide the body, Malone?"

The power of my stare actually made him back away. "They found someone?" I asked.

Then everyone was clustering around, wanting to tell me that I'd wasted my time. No, the police hadn't found a body on the rocks. Just the dog wandering close to the cliff, with no apparent reason for its show of distress. There had been no jumper on Berry Head that day. It was a false alarm.

Loser.

But that didn't stop the idiot Garvey saying, "Open his bag. Maybe he's got Freya's *heart* in there."

I'm not a violent kid, but I was so going to stuff Ryan's head down a drain, when a voice said, "Michael, I need to speak with you."

Maybe it was because it was a female voice. Or the haunting measure of authority it carried. Or perhaps it was the way she said *Meek-ell*, not *Mike-ell*, that made nine rowdy schoolboys turn as one animal.

"Wow." Ryan Garvey whistled.

For once, Mastermind spoke for us all.

She was across the road, leaning against a shining red scooter as slim and perfect in its breathtaking design as she was. Springs and brake hubs glinted in the sunlight; the mirrors stood up like two glass flags. The seat was so shiny and black that it looked for all the world like she'd only just torn off the shrink-wrap.

Stunning.

And so was she.

She must have been nineteen, maybe older. I'd have guessed she was French, even if I hadn't heard her speak. Spikes of short dark hair stabbed at the ridges of her prominent cheekbones. Her eyes were caramel brown and seemed to swirl at their center like the milky foam on a cappuccino. She was wearing a plain white dress. And on her feet were a pair of blue-and-white sneakers, their laces looped like butterfly wings. I had never really understood love at first sight. That day, I totally, *totally* got it.

She held out a helmet.

"Oh — my — God. Who is *she*?" Ryan hissed.

It took a few moments to find an answer. Under her riveting gaze, my mouth just didn't want to work anymore. A sudden crosswind picked up Garvey's notebook and blew it ten yards down the road, but even that couldn't shift his focus from the girl. Then, for no reason I could possibly imagine, other than that the words were just *there* in my head, I heard myself saying, "She's . . ." Another half second ticked by. The French girl gave me a nod of approval, as if she wanted me to speak my mind, no matter how weird the words might sound. And they *were* weird. "She's . . . the au pair."

"*What?*" said half a dozen guys at once.

She smiled like an early dawning light.

Ryan Garvey, BBC News, jabbed a finger in the girl's direction. "*She* seriously lives with you? She does things? Washes your boxers and stuff?"

It sounded credible. A French au pair. Everyone knew we weren't short of money.

So no one laughed.

And the girl just *stared*.

High in my skull, a school bell rang.

Almost immediately, she spoke again, guiding her gaze even deeper into mine, as if I were the toy she'd singled out and needed to grab from the arcade booth. "Michael, we have to go."

I looked dizzily at the helmet she was holding out to me. Black with a purple floral design. The patterns were wandering all over the dome.

Someone spat on the ground and said, "Come on, Malone. Stop messing around."

But I couldn't help myself. I stepped toward the girl and took the helmet.

She jumped on the scooter and sat astride it. "Get on. Hold my waist, okay?"

A small piece of me was crying *Danger! Danger!* but I swung my leg across the seat, laying my hands just above her hips. Despite her slender frame, her muscles felt taut and firm, like an athlete's. "Wh-where are you taking me?"

"That won't matter till we get there. Hold tight."

She kicked away the stand.

"*What?* What's he *doing?*" Garvey screeched. "Hambleton is gonna go nuts."

But the wind was already in my face, and school now seemed a tame alternative. We sped away, mocking the lines of traffic, and headed off into the flickering sunlight. I had no idea what was waiting for me. All I could think about was holding the girl and breathing her scent, which only seemed to add to her air of mystery — that and the creature inked on her shoulder. Just below the blowing collar of her dress was a small tattoo. As we slowed for a traffic light, I let go with one hand and touched a finger against the design, feeling the shock of her smooth white skin. She parted her lips and looked back, but said nothing. I took my hand away as we picked up speed, thinking about the book I'd been reading, how the tattoos found on *The Illustrated Man* were still by day but alive by night, foretelling grisly tales of death. What story did this creature tell? I wondered.

Who was the girl with the rearing black unicorn on her shoulder?

5 · BENCH

We left town and headed for the coast road again. Most of the way, I just did as I'd been told. I sat. I rode pillion. I held on to the girl. But as the salt air began to sting my cheeks, I woke up and gained some focus. I had been . . . abducted. Somehow mesmerized onto the scooter. I threw my head around as the memories came back, the tussle with the boys outside the school gates, the beautiful girl with the smooth French accent, the words she'd somehow put into my head: *au pair.*

I shouted, "Stop this. Who are you? Where are you taking me?"

The girl said, "Michael, be still," her voice ricocheting in the engine drone. I banged a fist twice against her shoulder. She cried out, "Hey!" and told me to stop. Her elbow jabbed back to keep me at bay.

"Let me go!" I shouted, already looking at the streaking road and wondering how much damage it would do to roll off, even in a floral-patterned helmet. I pounded her again.

She said something in French under her breath, then responded by tying the brakes into a knot and dragging the scooter through a low, tight arc. That answered my question well enough. It hurts like crazy when you fly off a bike. At least she'd had the grace to dump me on the grass.

I sat up, clutching my knee. One hand was slightly grazed. My left hip was on fire. I learned an important lesson that day: The prettiest girls can hurt you, and not always in the region of the heart.

"Take off your helmet. Don't think about running." She gunned the throttle as if she were holding a lion by the collar. And though the accent made her sound cute, there was no mistaking her dark intent.

I unstrapped the helmet. "Who are you? Why am I here?"

She tilted her head toward the sea.

We'd stopped on the same stretch of land where I'd caught the dog. Like yesterday, it was almost deserted — apart from the solitary figure of a man sitting on a bench, looking out to sea.

"Go. He wishes to speak with you."

I shook my head. "Why? Who is he?"

"Be sensible, Michael. Don't make me force you."

I clenched my fist, which only made her sigh. She turned off the scooter's engine and righted her hair with little nips of her fingers. "I am trained in four disciplines of the martial arts. I could tie you into a parcel if I wished and drop you on the seat beside him. Go, Michael. He does not like to be kept waiting. He told me to say he is a friend of your father."

It was clear from the unfeeling look in her eyes that she'd offered this line as a bargaining tool, a final persuader if all else failed. It had the desired effect. My stomach lurched and I was slightly sick. For three years, I'd waited for a moment like this, to meet someone who could help me rekindle the memories of a dad that time was eating away. Now it had happened, and here was the result: a pool of sick on the grass. The girl waited till I'd wiped my mouth, then she parked the scooter and beckoned me to stand, telling me to leave the helmet on the ground.

I thought about rushing her, but what were the chances? So I rose to my feet and headed toward the bench. The girl followed, keeping a reasonable distance, crossing her arms like a mother patrolling outside the school gates.

I approached the man slowly, coming close enough to hear a fob watch ticking in the pocket of his vest. He was sitting very upright with his hands on his knees, wearing a crisp black suit. His shoes were patent, also black. Thick-flowing layers of pale gray hair were combed back in watermelon lines across his scalp. From the color of the hair, I thought he might be elderly, but when I saw his face, I realized he couldn't have been more than thirty, if that. His features were sharp, almost highly machined, as if he'd been made by a 3-D printer.

"Such beauty," he said, "in so much emptiness." He spoke with a high-pitched German accent, a voice that seemed to complement his glacial cheekbones and alabaster skin. He patted the bench. "Please join me, Michael. I wish you no harm."

I lowered myself to a sitting position, keeping plenty of space between us.

He folded a newspaper onto his lap, last night's edition of the *Holton Post*. He clasped his hands across my photo, pressing the tips of his thumbs together. I noticed he was wearing a silver ring engraved with an image of a black unicorn. The same design the girl had tattooed on her shoulder, memorable not just for its color, but for a loop in the tail that looked like a lowercase letter *e*.

"My name is Amadeus Klimt," he said, as if he'd just read it off a passing cloud. "You may call me Mr. Klimt. Please forgive the abrupt manner in which you were brought here. I trust Chantelle treated you appropriately?"

I looked back at the girl, who now had a pretty name to match her fierce beauty. *Appropriately* was an interesting choice of word. It seemed to imply "by any means possible." In their world, that clearly included kidnapping. "She said you knew my father."

He raised his chin, letting his pale face bask in the warmth. "Yes. Your father was a very fine man. He worked for me — until he disappeared."

Right away, he'd blown his credibility. Dad had always worked for himself. He had traveled the world, demonstrating software for medical equipment. He didn't even have an office, just a spare room at home where he kept his paperwork. How could he possibly have worked for this man?

I kept my response as guarded as I could. "I don't remember Dad ever mentioning you." I looked again at Chantelle, hovering there, bored. I was wary now, thinking they were also journalists, attracted by my freakish rescue of the dog.

Mr. Klimt brushed a speck of dirt off his arm. "Your father would never have spoken of me, Michael. The organization I represent demands a high level of secrecy."

"You're from the government?"

"No, I am not." He looked up at a circling gull, tilting his head in admiration as though he'd never seen a bird in flight before. "Do you know what a 'nontemporal event' is?"

A *what*? I shook my head.

He stroked the newspaper, straightening my picture with the back of his hand. "I think such an event took place here yesterday. An episode of such unusual proportions that it cannot be explained by normal human mechanisms or environmental conditions. I'm referring, of course, to your adventure with the dog. I'd like to propose an exchange of information. You describe to me, in detail, what happened on this cliff top, and in return I will tell you more about your father."

"Where is he?"

"I don't know."

"Is he dead?"

"I don't think so. What do *you* believe?"

For the first time, he turned and looked at me. He had the strangest eyes I'd ever seen. They were a kind of washed-out purple color, set so far back into their shaded sockets, they looked like distant stars. It struck me, vaguely, that he could have been blind.

He smiled, waiting for an answer to his question. I shivered and looked out to sea. I hated thinking back to those awful days when Dad had not come home from his trip. The sleepless nights. The tears. The police. How a man called Mulrooney had eventually come around and talked to us over the lid of a briefcase. How he'd told us there were no reported problems with the flight, then, later, no ransom demands for a hostage. No passport had been found. No phone signal detected. Every lead they'd pursued had reached a dead end. Dad had vanished like a warm puff of smoke in the hot desert air. Another missing person. Case unsolved.

And as the days rolled into weeks, we knew in our hearts

he was never coming back. He was dead. What other explanation could there be? There were rumors suggesting he'd deserted us, that he'd forged a new identity and was living a false life, like a convict on the run. But I couldn't, and wouldn't, let myself believe that. This was the man who had read me countless bedtime stories, who'd made me a chain of paper dragons that still gathered dust around my bedpost at night. The man who, on returning from a trip, always stopped on the bottom porch step and kissed Mom, causing her to lift one foot into the air. Why would he betray us or ever let us down? He was gone, and no one knew what had happened to him, least of all this German stranger and his petulant, scooter-riding sidekick.

I jumped up and whipped my phone from my pocket. "Let me go or I'm calling the police."

Mr. Klimt seemed unconcerned. He studied me as if I were an act on a talent show.

"All I've got to do is dial 911."

"Then we both leave here with nothing," he said.

"I mean it." I started moving my thumb.

He raised his hand to reason with me.

At the same time, a shot rang out.

And the man I'd been talking to just seconds before slumped forward on the bench, a trail of blood running down his neck, staining the rim of his collarless shirt.

A black car had pulled up not far from Chantelle. The barrel of a rifle was pointing through its window. Chantelle shouted, "Run, Michael! Run!" Then another shot rang out and she spun around and crumpled to the grass, and was still.

Two men in dark glasses stepped out of the car. One shouted to the other, "Don't mess this up! We want the kid alive."

And that was when the strangeness happened again. As the fear welled up and my breathing quickened, the need to escape reached an unstoppable peak in my mind. My senses went crazy and I flashed toward the scooter. The next thing I knew, I was firing the ignition.

I heard their shouts, but by then I was away, cutting across the headland toward the group of houses that made up Coxborough village. I knew there was a narrow lane through to the green that even a small car couldn't have passed down. There would be people there. Tourists. Gift shops. The pub. I opened the throttle as wide as it would go, praying I wouldn't hit any rabbit holes or stones. I heard wheels spin behind me and knew the car was coming. Within half a minute, there'd be horsepower snorting down my neck. But if they wanted me alive, they were going to have to catch me. The chances were, I wouldn't get a bullet in the back.

At the entrance to the lane, I heard the squeal of their brakes. A fading horn blast signaled their annoyance. I didn't dare look back; I just kept on going. The gap was tight, but I didn't slow down. Over puddles and potholes I flew. I could see the green opening up in front of me. And I was almost there, almost clean away, when the scooter hit a mud bump and bucked like a lamb. I fought with the steering but couldn't stop the front end from pitching against a rough wooden fence. I scraped along, tearing my trousers at the knee, before hitting a clump of privet and finally flying off. The scooter slid into the adjoining road and crashed to a stop against a telephone pole. For the second time that day, I picked myself up from a painful fall. I had scratches on one side of my face from the privet. Other than that, I was sore but okay.

I limped into the open. Three people immediately rushed to the scene. One of them, mercy of mercies, was a policeman.

"Stand back," he ordered. "I'll deal with this." He caught me in his arms as I staggered forward. "Someone call an ambulance. He could be badly hurt. Heck, son, what were you playing at?"

"Murder," I panted.

"What?" he said.

"On the cliffs. They shot two people."

He steadied my face. "Who shot two people?"

"These men. Black car. They chased me to the lane."

He looked hard into my eyes. "Are you well enough to show me?"

I nodded. "I think so, yes."

"Okay, come with me."

With an arm around my shoulder, he guided me across to his waiting police car. He strapped me in, then reversed like a race-car driver and sped along the road that exited the village and circled back toward the headland. Barely thirty seconds later, I saw the black car.

"That's it," I said, pointing. "That's the car."

To my horror, the policeman headed straight for it.

"What are you doing?" I gasped. "No. They've got guns."

He said, "Calm down, Michael. There are no guns."

"Wha —? How do you know my name?"

He tore off a false mustache. That was when I realized I'd met him before. He was Mulrooney, the man who'd come to tell us about Dad's disappearance.

We pulled up beside the black car. Mulrooney jumped out and yanked my door wide open. The rear door of the black car also clicked open.

"Very impressive, Michael," said a voice. "Now please get in before you hurt yourself further. You're exhausted and your power will be weak."

I dipped my head and looked into the car.

There, in the backseat, was Amadeus Klimt.

"So, Michael, do we have a deal?"

The car pulled away smoothly. Klimt pressed a button on the armrest beside him, and a screen came up between us and the driver. "Let me remind you. It's really very simple. You explain to me how you rescued the dog, and I give you information about your father."

"You were dead," I said, still a little freaked out. The bloodstain was right there on his shirt.

He laced his fingers, moving his hands like a party clown about to make animal shadows. "In my line of business, things are rarely what they seem."

"What is your *business*?"

"We will come to that."

I tried to look out the window, but the glass was tinted on the inside surface. Whoever these people were, they liked their secrecy. "Where's Chantelle? Is she okay?"

"Chantelle has returned to her duties. She will be angry about the scooter. You may have to deal with the consequences of that."

Like it was *my* fault she'd driven me into their charade. "Where are you taking me?"

"Home," he said plainly. "We are driving you home. How long the journey takes will be entirely dependent upon our discussion."

I sighed and looked at the state of my clothing. For the second day running, my uniform was ruined. There was a rip in the sleeve of my jacket, too. Mom was going to go absolutely mental. A year driving around Holton Byford probably wouldn't be long enough to calm her down. "I need to be in school. Take me there instead." At school I could cook up some feeble story that might just scrape under Hambleton's radar and give me time to clean off some dirt. But Klimt quashed that in his very next sentence.

"Chantelle has already reported your truancy."

"*What?*"

"You will be punished, of course, but that may yet have a positive outcome."

I slammed back into my seat. "Tell her thanks — for nothing!"

"You may tell her yourself next time you see her."

Next time? Never would be far too soon. This was payback for the scooter, no doubt. Now Mom and Hambleton would both be on my case. "How did you know I'd go down the lane? Does everyone in Coxborough work for you?"

He took a sip of blue-colored fluid through a straw dipped into a plastic vessel. A slight smell of menthol filled the air. Whatever he was drinking, it wasn't water. "Our meeting, as I'm sure you'll appreciate, was staged. I knew you'd be reluctant to share your . . . experience, so I decided to provoke a repeat performance. The guns and the blood were merely illusions, designed to test your emotional response to a dangerous situation. There were only three ways you could have escaped: left or right along the cliffs, or down the lane to Coxborough. Along the cliffs, you would have been caught by the car. It was a simple matter to position an agent on the far side of the lane in a guise you would quickly submit to and trust."

Opening a compartment on the armrest between us, he picked out an orange and a bright white napkin. He placed the napkin over his lap, then proceeded to peel the orange skin onto it. "Would you like one, Michael?"

I shook my head. I didn't do fruit, especially not the messy ones. And for all I knew, it might have been spiked with a truth drug or something. "I remember Mulrooney. He came to our house."

Mr. Klimt nodded. "He and your father were colleagues, and friends. On another day, it could have been Mulrooney on that plane to New Mexico. Then I might have been talking to *his* son instead."

"You mean, you sent Dad on some kind of *mission*?"

I watched him put an orange segment onto his tongue, taking it in like a lizard would a fly. He swallowed it whole, didn't appear to chew. "Your father was not a salesman, Michael. That was also an illusion. A cover to protect the true nature of his work. Of course, you are going to question this. But consider my line of reasoning first: If your father was all you believed him to be, he or his body would have been returned to you. That is the likeliest conclusion if a man goes missing when his sole occupation is selling computer programs to medical establishments. My account brings you a new kind of hope. Hope that he's alive. Hope that you will find him. You may be the only person who can."

I looked away, wondering if I might be dreaming. How could Dad have lived a false life and none of us known a thing about it? "What did he do? Was he some kind of spy?"

"Yes, in a manner of speaking. He used his abilities to investigate things that did not make sense. Things that go 'bump in the night,' you might say."

"Are you telling me Dad was a *ghost* hunter?"

Klimt flapped a dismissive hand. "That would be a minor strand of our work. Unexplained incidents, cryptic occurrences, and relative nontemporal events. That is what we investigate." He produced a business card from his jacket and held it between his first two fingers.

Hesitantly, I took it from him. The only word on it was *UNICORNE*, in embossed silver letters that almost disappeared into the white of the card. Below the name was the image of the rearing black unicorn. I couldn't understand at first why an *E* had been added to the end of *UNICORN*. Then I worked out that the looping *e* in the tail of the horse was there for exactly that reason. I also began to see an acronym in the name. UNexplained Incidents, Cryptic Occurrences . . . even down to the final three letters. "What *is* a Relative Nontemporal Event?" I remembered his mentioning this on the bench.

He put the remainder of the orange aside and patted his lips with a corner of the napkin. "Tell me what happened with the dog. This is your side of the agreement. It does not matter how ridiculous it seems. I have encountered many strange phenomena in my time. Please, hold nothing back."

So I told him what I knew, or what I could remember. Everything from the asthma diagnosis to sensing the husky's thoughts and rescuing it. I spoke for several minutes, and in all that time, he never interrupted, as if he had a tape recorder running in his head. Finally, when I was beginning to ramble, he held up a hand to tell me to stop.

"Was this the first occasion you'd experienced such a shift?"

Shift? What was that supposed to mean? "Um, yes. I think so."

He synchronized his fingertips and tapped them together. "Have you spoken to anyone else about this?"

I shook my head.

"What about the journalists?"

I lifted my shoulders. "They asked some questions and took some stuff from my sister's phone, but —"

"Photographs?"

"Yes. But they were useless. Blurred."

He made a slight humming sound as he traced the angle of his throat with a finger, his purple eyes fixed on the space in front of him.

"We didn't give permission."

"It does not matter," he said, without moving his gaze. And then he changed the subject. "Tell me something; be as honest as you can. Do you ever think you sense your father's presence?"

That made me sigh. I rolled my head against my shoulder and tried to look out the window again. So many times since Dad's disappearance I'd walked past his room, hoping he'd spring out and hug my shoulders. "Want to go outside and kick a ball around, Mikey?" That was the kind of thing he would say. That was the dad I knew and loved. The dad I remembered. The dad I wanted back. But did I ever sense him? No, not really. I said to Klimt, "Why are you asking me this? What's Dad got to do with me saving the dog?"

He picked out his fob watch and checked the time. "Please answer the question, Michael."

"No," I said irritably. "No, I don't *feel* him." I crossed my arms tight, smothering the need to strike at something. I'd tried so hard to shut all of this out, the aggression I felt toward Dad sometimes, the blame I attached to him for letting us down. "How did you get him?"

"Get him?" Klimt repeated.

"How did he come to work for you? What could he do, this dad I never knew?"

Klimt tapped a finger against his thigh. It seemed to mesmerize me slightly, like a dripping tap. "Your father was a talented software engineer. We heard about him from another source and engaged him to work on a new design project. He was so far ahead of others in his field that we invited him into our UNICORNE facility, where he agreed to take some tests. We soon discovered a number of remarkable talents. For instance, he could accurately gauge an individual's mood and know, with certainty, if they were lying or telling the truth. This is a valuable skill to possess — especially when probing accounts of paranormal activity."

"How?" I asked. "How did he do it?"

"He was able to detect minute variations in the pigmentation of a person's iris, the circle of the eye that is colored. He called it *flecking*. Try it sometime, on someone you trust."

"You think *I* could tell when people are lying?"

"With training, yes. But that is just the tip of your . . . potential, Michael. I believe you have inherited your father's abilities but taken them to new and higher levels. Do you know what a multiverse is?"

This sounded like physics. Not my best subject.

Klimt read my face and smiled. "I will explain," he said. "Some scientists believe that our world is made up of an infinite number of universes, linked so closely that a simple decision — say, choosing to eat an orange or not — might involve our entering a parallel universe and setting off a whole new chain of events. If I eat the orange, for instance, I might spill some of the juice onto my suit. So I decide to take the suit to be cleaned, and as I'm crossing the road to the dry cleaner, I'm hit by a bus. Do you see what I'm getting at?"

"None of this happens if you don't eat the orange."

"Correct. But the possibility that it could happen is always present somewhere in the multiverse."

"So . . . ?"

"So imagine you had the power to affect the multiverse, to rearrange its layers to achieve a desired outcome."

"That would make you . . . king of the world," I said.

"A little poetic, but yes. And what if I told you you'd done this twice — as easily as flipping through the pages of a book?"

I snorted a laugh. Okay, some weird stuff had happened in the last two days. But hopping between universes? That sort of thing only worked in comics. "That's crazy. No one can mess with . . . the future."

"Then we need to continue driving," he said, "until you are convinced. Meanwhile, there is one thing I can tell you with certainty."

"What's that?"

"You do not have asthma."

"It's really quite simple to understand," said Klimt as the car continued its circuit of Holton. "Yesterday, on this headland, you made contact with the raw emotions of an animal, one so deeply distressed that you suspected it was ready to leap off a cliff. You pictured yourself saving it. Am I correct?"

"Yes, but —"

"In that moment, when your level of concern for the dog was so great, something quite extraordinary happened. Somehow, you separated your imagined reality from your physical one. You followed the path of your projected thoughts and created the outcome you desired to see happen. We have a word for this: We call it *imagineering*."

"So I . . . what . . . traveled through time?"

"Momentarily, yes. I believe your consciousness moved to a future point just ahead of the dog's intended leap. To complete the action, your physical body then needed to catch up so the time frames might be realigned. To an external observer, it would appear that you vanished from one location and instantly materialized in another. This was reflected in the words of the policeman who was interviewed at the scene."

A superhuman force, he'd said. It made my skin prickle just thinking about it.

"And Dad could do this?"

"Yes, but it was flawed and unpredictable. We believe your father might have 'traveled' in the same way you did — but the time frames somehow failed to realign."

"You mean . . . he's lost in time?"

"That would be the simplest way of putting it, yes. Now, I need to ask you something important. Think carefully before you answer. This may require intense concentration. Since the original shift, have you noticed any changes in your circumstances? Anything unusual, no matter how small?"

At first I was going to tell him no. Apart from saving the dog and playing witness to a fabricated double murder, the last two days had been pretty average.

Then I remembered Josie and the flute.

I told him about the flute case and her school rehearsal. How Josie telling the police about her music exam was the last thing I'd been thinking of before I went after the dog.

Once again, he stared into the middle distance, as if his

brain was searching for another gear. "Yet you seem to recollect that, until this time, your sister had no talent for the instrument?"

"I think so. I don't know. It's kind of hard to remember." Like a crumb falling off the edge of a plate. "She does play now, though. She's really good."

"Fascinating," he said. His left eye flickered, not unlike an LED on a computer. "Your sister's invention has become a valid part of your altered reality. That is quite a feat."

He leaned forward and tapped the screen. The barrier stayed up, but the deepening hum from the automatic gearbox suggested we were done and I would now be taken home.

"Is that it?" I said. I felt a little cheated. I had told him a lot; he had told me very little.

"Yes," he said. "You may return to your family."

"But . . . what about Dad?"

"What about him, Michael?"

"You said I could find him. What do I do?"

"Nothing," he said. "You do nothing about your father, unless we request it. UNICORNE will continue the search for now."

So why was I even in the car? "No. I need to know where he is, Mr. Klimt. You have to let me help you. You have to. Please."

"And how do you propose I go about this?"

"Do tests. Whatever. Like you did with Dad. Let me be a part of your organization. Make me a member of UNICORNE."

He looked down into his lap and smiled. "You would be a boy in an unsafe world. You have no idea what dangers could await you."

"I don't care. I'll do anything to get Dad home. Let me prove myself to you. Give me a mission. There must be something I can do."

The car rolled to a halt.

"Please, Mr. Klimt."

His eyes looked up to a gap in the screen, a signal to the driver not to open the door yet. "Very well," he said. "I will give you a task. But there are rules, Michael. Serious rules. If you break them, you will put yourself in jeopardy, and all chance of finding your father will be gone. There are people out there, other organizations, who would stop at nothing to access your abilities. This episode with the dog will not have gone unnoticed."

I gulped and gave a quick nod.

"Rule number one. You do not speak about UNICORNE to anyone, not even to your family, and certainly not to your friends. Anything you find, you share only with me, Chantelle, or Mulrooney. Do I have your word on this?"

"Yes. Where do I start?"

"Find out about the dog."

The dog? No evil villains or burning helicopters or secret underground particle colliders? Just find out about the stupid *dog*? "Why? What for?"

"There is a reason it was alone on the cliff. Something about that dog triggered a powerful reaction in you. I'm interested to know what made you connect."

He nodded at the screen. My door clicked open.

"But . . . it was just a dog, being a dog and stuff."

"That is all, Michael. Now you may go — unless you'd like my driver to haul you out?" He pointed to the outside world.

I sighed and stepped out of the car. But before they could close their automated door, there was one more question I needed to ask, perhaps the biggest question of all. "What was Dad's mission? Why did UNICORNE send him to New Mexico?"

"Good-bye, Michael," Mr. Klimt said. "I'll contact you again when the moment is right. Oh, one last word of warning: Be careful what you wish for — it might come true."

"Wait!" I cried as the door clicked shut. "How do I contact you if I need to? And how am I supposed to find Chantelle?" But by then the car was halfway up the road. And Amadeus Klimt was gone.

They had dropped me off behind a sprawling hedge, fifty yards away from the side of our house. My uniform, although it had dried out a little, was still in a terrible state. There was nothing else for it but to go and face Mom.

I didn't even make it as far as the front door.

Halfway up the drive, she appeared on the step.

"Mom," I began.

"Don't even try. Just get inside, get upstairs, and get those clothes off. You are in *such* deep trouble, young man. I've had the *school* on the phone, the *police* have been here, and that photographer from the paper has been sniffing around again."

"Eddie? What did he want?"

"I don't know, Michael. And I don't really care. What in heaven's name were you thinking of, taking the scooter like that?"

"Mom, I — How did you know I'd been on the scooter?"

"Don't test my patience," she threatened. "Inside. Upstairs. Shower. Now."

And really, what was the point of arguing?

I dragged myself past her, half expecting a slap around my ear. But all I could feel was her disappointed shudder. If only I could tell her.

What a day.

I clumped upstairs, pulling off my tie and loosening my jacket. As I turned on the landing, I walked past the bathroom, where I would be spending the next twenty minutes trying to find a way to sluice myself into a gutter, no doubt.

Precisely one step past the bathroom door, I stopped, rocked back, and pushed the door open.

She gave me a look that suggested she'd like to rip out my heart with a garlic press.

"What are *you* doing here?" I gasped.

She scowled and replied, "What does it look like?"

It looked like Chantelle, being an au pair.

Folding my boxers into a pile to be washed.

At first glance, my life was exactly the same as it had been just before I'd taken the scooter. My toothbrush was still in its place on the rack. My soccer cleats had a large hole in the toe. My secret stash of quarters was huddled in a sock at the back of my drawer. Everything was how it ought to be. Normal. But, as with Josie and the flute, changes had been made. They were all built around the thoughts I'd been holding at the forefront of my mind when I'd gone through the "shift" that Klimt had talked about — the need to escape from the men in dark glasses, and the weird idea that Chantelle was our au pair. To use his words, she was now "a valid part of my altered reality."

Fantastique? Not.

She had the spare room at the top of the stairs but shared our space like the big moody sister any self-respecting boy would have gladly locked away in the attic on a bet. She didn't want to talk about Klimt or the scooter (in the garage for repairs to its bodywork and mirror), other than to say that if I ever took a "joyride" on it again, she would do unspeakable things to me. The threat was delivered in a huffy form of French, most of which I worked out by inference. I might have imagineered these cozy domestic circumstances for her, but it hadn't improved her Gallic sulks. Under pressure, I did question the joyride element, only for Mom to wade in hard and accuse me of stealing the bike to show off. My "fame," she accused me, had gone to my head. And the weird thing was, it all made sense. The more they gave of their version of events, the more it reinforced the new reality, and the harder it became to remember (or believe) what used to be. By the end of the day, it felt as though Chantelle had always been part of the family, chatting about Paris and fashion with Josie and easing the full-time burden on Mom. I might have stepped into a parallel universe, but it was an incredibly familiar one that everyone around me was comfortable with.

There were repercussions, of course. I would be grounded for "as long as it took," and a large portion of my weekly allowance would go to Chantelle until the repair costs were fully paid back. That was fine. I could deal with that. What I found so much harder to accept was that my whole relationship with Mom had turned sour. An invisible line had been drawn between us. I was now the "hormonal" son. I'd earned myself the label "troublesome teen."

At school, that point was hammered home with venom. My first stop the next morning was not chemistry with Mr.

Boland but an audience with Mr. Solomon, the principal, a man who had very little "chemistry" with anything but orcs, hobgoblins, and gargoyles.

He didn't seem to care about my taking the scooter. If I wanted to kill myself or rack up an adolescent criminal record, that was my silly business, he said. For him, it was all about dishonoring the school and the sudden deviation from the norm. He, too, had read about my "stunt" on the cliff. In the space of twenty-four hours, I'd gone from model pupil to juvenile delinquent. I was offered the chance to explain myself. I couldn't. The first rule of UNICORNE was you did not talk about UNICORNE, right? So I acted the part of the sullen schoolboy and grunted and shrugged and pretended to be bored. Then came the lecture, followed by the punishment. It was mild.

"I'm giving you a verbal warning. Any repeat of this behavior will mean a suspension. A formal letter will be sent to your mother. Now get out."

Thank you very much, Chantelle.

I stepped out of the office, dragging what was left of my pride behind me. And who should be in the corridor, waiting, but . . .

"Freya!" I gasped.

She stared through her spikes of gelled black hair. She really was everything the other kids joked about. A moody, disaffected, shabbily dressed girl with a face the color of vanilla sorbet. The skin beneath her eyes was sagging like a curtain coming off its rail. She looked as if she hadn't slept for a year, but at least she hadn't died at the bottom of a cliff (unless Garvey had been right about the vampire thing).

Mrs. Greaves, the principal's secretary, walked past en route to the photocopier. She tapped Freya's shoulder and said, "Your turn."

Freya rolled out her tongue and removed a wad of limp gray gum from her mouth. Out of sight of Mrs. Greaves, she pressed it behind the stump of a yucca plant. I smiled, wondering if she'd pick it up when she was through with Solomon. "What have you done?" I whispered.

She stuck her chin in the air and turned her gaze away. But there was just enough interest in her tired brown eyes to encourage me to ask, "Is Trace okay?"

By then, she had slouched into Solomon's office, and Mrs. Greaves was giving me grief. "Don't you have a lesson to go to, Michael?"

The photocopier flared. "Yes, ma'am."

"Then go."

It was almost morning break by the time Freya made it to the chemistry lab. She parked herself on a bench near the back, hidden behind a couple of tall burettes. She stared out the window for the remaining eight minutes of the lesson. Mr. Boland noticed her, but let it pass. Freya was a lost cause to most of the staff.

But she was the key to my progress with UNICORNE. So when the bell for recess sounded, I shoved Ryan and the rest of the crew aside and quietly followed Freya out of school. She went deep into the grounds, on a winding walk across the soccer field, before slumping in a heap on a well-carved tree stump surrounded by a crop of dandelions. The journey had taken her almost five minutes, which was a measure of her loneliness, I thought. I approached slowly, making sure my footfalls were heavy enough so she wouldn't think I was creeping up. Her forehead was sunk against her forearms in her lap. I was fairly close in before she murmured, "Leave me alone, whoever you are."

"It's me."

Silence.

"Michael. Malone."

More silence.

Awkward.

"Hey, Freya," I began.

She said, "I don't date and no, you can't copy my biology homework."

It took me several seconds to realize this was a pretty slick joke. First surprise: Freya had a sense of humor. She also had limited patience.

"Whatever tired joke you're playing won't work. I'm immune to insults and idiots like Garvey. Get lost, Malone. I don't drink blood, but I sure can bite."

I crouched down and snapped a blade of grass. "I just wanted to know if Trace was okay. Neat name, by the way. Did you call him that?"

"It's a her," she tutted.

A husky female. There was a wisecrack there, but I didn't pursue it. Instead, I said dumbly, "Yeah, well, it was . . . misty."

"*What?*" She lifted her face off her hands.

I shrugged and flicked away the blade of grass. "Guess you were right: Biology isn't my strongest subject."

Drumroll. Muted cymbal crash. *Thank you, I'll be here all week.* Smug me thought that was a smart reply to her homework gag, but when she looked me in the eye, she wasn't smiling. "You faked it, didn't you?"

"Sorry? Faked what?"

"No one could have held Trace still that long."

Oh, the photograph. "The photographer tricked me. Don't believe everything you see in the papers."

"I don't — or anything I read. Trace is a wolf in doggy fur. There's no way a wimp like you could have caught her as easily as they said."

"Me and my uniform disagree, sorry. You want to see the dry cleaning bill?"

She spat out another chunk of gum. "You're a real comedian, aren't you?"

"Hey. Chill out. I didn't come looking for a fight, okay?"

"Good. You'd lose." She got up and stormed toward the school buildings.

A second lapsed, then I let myself snap. "She was going to jump."

I heard Freya's footsteps slow to a stop.

"I can't explain how I knew, I just did. So I ran for her. It all happened fast, in a blur. I didn't know the journalists were going to turn up or what they were going to do with the picture. I swear, I hardly spoke to them. They made up all that stupid stuff about me having 'superpowers.' You might like to know that I don't own a cape and I keep my underwear *inside* my trousers."

She snorted at that. A slight thaw, perhaps? I took a chance and looked over my shoulder at her. She was standing by a goalpost, stubbing her toe against it. "I like dogs, Freya. That's all there is to it."

She nodded, but didn't speak.

"Why was Trace loose on the headland that morning?"

I was confident I'd get a reply, and I did. I was working out where on my wimpy body I could have my secret UNICORNE tattoo, when Freya blew the dream far across the playing fields. "I don't know," she mumbled.

"How come? You must know."

"Why?"

"Because . . ." I spread my hands. "Did you leave the back door open or something?"

"Um, no?" She hit me with her trademark sneer.

"She got off the leash, then?"

"Malone, let it go."

"It's a simple question, Freya. How come Trace was running the cliff?"

"I don't *know*," she shouted, loud, like she was scared.

The bell rang for the end of recess.

"But that doesn't make sense. Either you —"

"Jeez," she cut in. "Are you totally dumb?" She bit her lip and seemed a little freaked out. "I don't know why she was on the cliffs — Trace is not my dog, okay?"

"*What?*"

"Oh!" With a sigh, she hurried away, walking briskly with her shoulders hunched and her arms tightly folded.

I caught up with her by the grassy embankment that sloped down from the playing fields toward the school drive. "Freya, wait." I took her lightly by the arm.

"Get off me!" She turned and flapped her hands.

Someone grunted, "Fight!" and an audience of kids seemed to instantly materialize on the drive.

"If Trace is not your dog, whose is she?"

More flapping. "Just leave me alone!"

"Freya, will you —" I grabbed her wrists and shook her till she looked at me. "The girl, the reporter, she said she was yours."

"Well, she was wrong. Let me *go*."

"But you know something, don't you? You're just afraid to say." I could see the sparks of fear in her eyes.

"I'm gonna scream," she threatened.

And, boy, could she holler. An eardrum-shattering howl that rattled the school windows and drove a gang of crows out of the nearby trees.

The kids on the driveway whooped and cheered.

Not so Mr. Besson, my languages teacher, who bellowed at me from an open window. "Michael Malone! What do you think you're doing?"

So I let Freya go, raising my hands as if the cops had the drop on me. Instantly, she lost her footing and stumbled backward down the slope. It wasn't steep and the ground here was dry, but it didn't do a lot for her fading dignity — or my tarnished image.

"Freya!" I called, and scrambled down after her.

Right away she was swamped by kids. Some of them wanted to check she wasn't hurt, but most were just taking a ghoulish peek at the traumatized goth girl rocking back and forth like a frightened animal, sobbing into her shaking hands.

"Out of the way. All of you. Now." Mr. Besson was there in moments, peeling kids aside in an effort to get through.

"It was him, sir. He pushed her." The fingers came for me.

"Sir, I —"

"Be quiet," snapped Besson. "I'll deal with you later. I said, stand *back*. Give the girl some air."

He knelt beside Freya, tucking his tie into the belt of his trousers as though contact with it might shatter her into pieces. "Freya, it's Mr. Besson. Are you hurt?"

"Just leave me alone," she sobbed.

"You know I can't do that. I need you to stand and come with me to the office. Have you knocked your head?"

She shook it hard. But through the gaps of her fingers I could see what Mr. Besson could see: the first signs of a bruise developing. Gently, he pulled one hand away. On her left temple was a dull red mark. It was about the size of a quarter and looked like a spill of wine on a tablecloth. I couldn't understand it. I'd watched her fall all the way to the bottom and I was pretty sure she hadn't struck her head on the drive.

But Mr. Besson was taking no chances. He gently pulled Freya to her feet and guided her away. Over his shoulder, he said, "Malone, you'd better follow — at a sensible distance."

So I dropped in behind them, feeling like a prisoner on the walk to his cell. Kids were speaking abuse from all sides, and Mr. Besson was doing nothing to stop them. Finally, we got inside and everything calmed. As we approached the office, even Freya was beginning to play down what had happened. "Sir, I'm all right." I heard her fussing. "I don't want this. I'll be fine. I'm okay. Really." And, "I slipped, sir. It wasn't Malone's fault."

"Well, we still need to look at that injury," he said. "Wait there a moment." He knocked on the office door and went straight in, giving me a chance to be alone with Freya.

"I'm sorry," I said, sidling up. I had my hands in my pockets, head bent low.

"Go away," she whispered, covering her face. She scrubbed her fingers through her raggedy hair. Despite the relative safety of reception, she seemed more troubled here than she had been on the field.

I chewed my lip. "I can't, you heard Besson. Is your head okay?"

"Don't look at me," she squealed, turning away. And then she said something very strange, something I didn't think was meant for me. "Please, get out of my head. . . ."

Half a second to respond. And Besson was coming back. "Who?" I asked quietly. "Who's in your head?" I tried to touch her arm, but she batted me away. At the same time, the office door opened and Mr. Besson called her in. As she moved across to the doorway, I glanced at her face — and saw something that made me start. Her left temple was normal and clear.

The red mark that had been there had completely disappeared.

"Suspended?"

"Mom, I swear, I didn't do anything."

"Suspended?" she repeated, in the way someone would if you told them aliens had stolen your laundry. Her confusion filled the living room like invisible dark energy.

Josie stared at me, openmouthed. "Tirion said you had a fight with Freya."

"Fight?!" Mom's words were growing harsher by the vowel.

"It wasn't a *fight*. And who the heck is Tirion?"

"My new friend," Josie said. "What did you do to Freya?"

"Nothing. I did nothing."

Chantelle came in and leaned against the door frame.

"We were arguing and she slipped. I didn't push her or hit her. Ask her yourself. Solomon suspended me because . . ."

"Because?" said Mom.

I had to look away from her; I couldn't find the words. But all of a sudden, they were pouring out of Mom. "Because he's run out of patience. And so have I. What on earth has happened to you, Michael? Ever since this . . . scrimmage with the dog, you've become every mother's worst nightmare. You used to be so . . ."

"Sweet," Josie said, raising an eyebrow.

In another reality, maybe.

"I dread to think what your father would have said."

And oh, how I would have loved to tell Mom that Dad was the reason I was putting myself through this. Dad, who seemed even more distant to me now. I glanced at Chantelle, who was airily posed, there to make sure I kept my mouth shut about Amadeus Klimt and UNICORNE, no doubt.

"How long?" Mom said. "How many days before you go back?"

"Three," I mumbled.

"*How* many?" gasped Mom.

"Three. I just said so, didn't I?"

"Don't you talk back at me, young man." Mom's glare became laser intense. "Well, you will work," she said, poking my shoulder. "You will stay in your room with your head in your textbooks and you will demonstrate to me that you are truly sorry for the hurt and embarrassment you've brought to this family. While I'm at work and Josie is at school, Chantelle will bring you your meals and —"

"Mom —?"

"Be quiet, I haven't finished. You will stay up there for the whole three days so you know what it means to be deprived of your freedom and other comforts. And it begins right now." She pointed to the stairs.

"Mom, please."

"Go, Michael."

Josie made hamster hands across her mouth. This was serious stuff. Her once "sweet" brother was effectively under house arrest.

I picked up my bag and sloped toward the door. Chantelle said to Mom, "The garage called. I'm going to fetch the scooter." She moved aside to let me pass. But in the moment it took to get a waft of her scent, she got the message I was silently mouthing.

We need to talk.

Maybe when she brought me my first bowl of *porridge*.

In fact, Josie was the first one I saw. Two hours had limped by and I had done precisely nothing but watch raindrops roll down my bedroom window. I was rapidly discovering that changing my reality carried its downfalls as well as its perks. Or maybe I was just feeling sorry for myself because I hadn't gotten to the root of my "mission"? If I couldn't solve some silly little mystery about a dog, how would I ever find my way to Dad? I was turning his paper chain of dragons through my hands when Josie knocked on the door and eased her way in. She marched across the room, stood on tiptoe so she could reach around my neck, and gave me a hug. "Night-night," she whispered, and turned away.

"Jose, don't go."

She paused by the door, curling and uncurling her fingers. I was guessing Mom had ordered her not to speak to me, but there had always been enough of the rebel in Josie to do what she thought was right. "Mom'll kill me if she finds me here."

"I know."

"I can't stay."

"Will you do something for me?"

She looked toward the landing.

"Please?"

She closed the door a little so Mom couldn't hear. "What?"

"Talk to Freya for me."

"*Michael?*"

"She's scared, Josie. Something's wrong about the dog. Freya says it's not hers, but talking about it turns her loopy."

"Not hers? But they said in the paper . . . ?"

"I know, but Freya says different. That's what we were . . . arguing about."

She sighed and hunched her shoulders. "Why would she talk to me, sister of the boy who gave her grief?"

"I think she wants to tell someone what she knows."

"And what does she know?"

"That's what I need you to find out, *Sherlock*. Just, y'know, be a girl. Make friends with her."

"Trick-or-treat with the goth freak? Thanks." She threw her hair behind one ear. "Would, but can't."

"Why not?"

"Because she's *older* than me."

"So?"

"So she wouldn't be seen dead with a fifth grader, dimwit."

I looked down at my hands and had an idea. "Tell her you like dragons."

"Dragons? Is this a joke?"

"Ryan says she draws them."

Her face filled with disbelief. "Anything that comes from Ryan Garvey's mouth came straight out of a clown manual first."

"Honestly, she likes them. I've seen her with *The Hobbit*."

"That's about funny little men with hairy feet, Michael."

"There's a dragon in it, too. Just talk to her, Jose. Honestly, she's not as bad as people say. She's . . . quite smart, actually."

"Oh, now I get it. You 'like' her, don't you?" She made quote marks with her fingers.

"What? Don't be dumb. I don't like *Freya*."

Josie just grinned and patted her cheeks, meaning mine were glowing like coals. Where were the shadows in this room when you needed them? "Look, just find out anything you can. Hambleton said she had an operation."

"Oh, nice topic when you finally start dating! You show me your scars and I'll show you mine? Why are you so interested, anyway?"

"In what?"

"Freya, the dog, any of it?"

I rubbed a paper dragon between my thumb and fingers. Could I afford to make Josie part of this? Klimt's orders had been pretty clear. No mentions of UNICORNE to anyone. Thankfully, I was spared a decision when Chantelle called out from downstairs, "*Josie, est-ce que tu veux un chocolat chaud ce soir?*"

Josie immediately scampered away to the bathroom. She flushed the toilet and quickly called back, "Sorry, did you ask me something?"

She frowned at me as she flashed past my room and hurried downstairs. And though she hadn't confirmed it either way, somehow I knew I could count on her help.

I didn't see Chantelle until the following morning. Mom came in briefly with a breakfast tray and repeated the terms of my imprisonment. But I was on my game by then and had schoolbooks open on the floor and on my desk. Mom said before she left, "I do love you, Michael, and I always will. Please don't test the extent of it."

And that actually made me cry a little.

I was still crumpling a tissue when Chantelle knocked on my door and flowed into the room. She arranged herself on my battered desk chair, with one leg tucked under her. She was wearing slacks and a sloppy gray sweater, but she still looked cool and French and — amazing. "So," she said, gazing at my poster of a Lamborghini Gallardo, "you've been a bad boy, Michael." She picked up a pencil and bridged it between her manicured fingers. "Klimt will not be impressed."

"Is that why you're here, to tell me I'm finished?"

"You said you wanted to talk. Here I am. Talk."

"The dog doesn't belong to Freya."

"And this is supposed to be meaningful to me?" She angled her free foot into the air.

"Klimt told me to report everything to you."

"And this is all you have to tell me, that the dog does not belong to Freya?" She lifted a page of my history book and let it fall like a dying swan. "I have work to do. I'll return at noon, possibly with a sandwich — if your behavior is good."

She stood up and so did I. Even though I was several years younger than her, I was tall enough to block her path.

She smiled and spiraled a hand toward my face, dragging a nail slowly down my cheek. I was so tense I thought my skin would split. She said, "Are you sure you want to confront me, Michael? You may have some interesting powers, but you know I could easily glamour you again."

Glamour me? Wasn't that what vampires did to their victims? I felt a vein twitching in the side of my neck. "It's not just the dog; there's something odd about the girl. I need Klimt's help. How do I contact him?"

"You don't. Klimt comes to you, when he's ready."

"Well, in case you hadn't noticed, I'm holed up in my bedroom. He's hardly going to pop by and help me write my essay on the Civil War, is he?"

She glanced down at my bed, where my cell phone had beeped. "You have a text. Maybe it's from her, the girl?"

She reached for the door handle, but I beat her to it. "Tell me your story."

"This is not wise, Michael."

"How did you get involved with UNICORNE? How long have you worked for them?"

Her gaze faltered for a moment, as if it would pain her to reveal the truth. "That is not your concern."

"Who are they, Chantelle? What do they do?"

"You know what they do. They investigate mysteries. They use people like me to find the truth. Now step away from the door, or I *will* hurt you."

I stood aside and let her go, but not without throwing in one last question. "Did you know my father?"

She paused and rocked back, taking time to fold her arms. "No," she said quietly. And then she was gone.

After a moment or two, I yanked up the phone and read the text. It wasn't from Freya. It was from Ryan Garvey. A stupid picture of me hanging from a gallows, with the message *Enjoy your suspension, loser.* I threw the phone down.

Not long afterward, it rang again.

And rang and rang.

Unknown caller.

I hit the button.

"Hello, Michael," said a voice.

Amadeus Klimt.

I did that all-in-one twisting thing and sank onto the bed, with the phone to my ear. "I'm at home," I said. I couldn't think of anything else to tell him.

"Yes," he said in his strangely detached German accent. "Chantelle has been updating me."

And why didn't that surprise me? Biting my tongue about all things French, I took a sharp breath and said, "I tried to talk to a girl called Freya. I thought she owned the dog, but she doesn't. It all went wrong, but I'm sure she knows something. I've asked my sister to speak to her. I haven't said anything about UNICORNE, I promise."

Silence. I imagined him peeling another orange or picking the seeds out of a pomegranate. I rolled onto my back and let my eyes scan the ceiling. Stuck to the plaster above my bed was a rocket ship, a moon, and a flurry of stars. Dad had put them up there before I was born. After his disappearance, I used to cry myself to sleep when the lights went out, watching the pieces fluoresce in the emptiness like tiny reminders of him. It occurred to me now that it had been a long time since I'd noticed them.

Klimt said, "How do you plan to use your confinement?"

"I don't know," I sighed. "Please don't take me off the mission."

"Do you believe there is something interesting to discover, something worthy of a UNICORNE file?"

"Yes. There's definitely something weird about Freya. I saw this mark on her head that came up like a bruise but had disappeared the next time I looked at her."

"Can you be sure it was not a shadow? Light can be very deceptive, Michael."

Now he was making me doubt what I'd seen. Perhaps it was a dirt stain and she'd rubbed it off during the walk to the office? But dirt stains didn't look red on the skin. And what was all that fuss about someone in her head?

Klimt spoke again. "Let these thoughts about Freya rest for now. Instead, ask yourself this: What do you most need to know about the dog?"

That wasn't hard to answer; the question had kept me awake all night. "Who it really belongs to," I muttered.

"Correct," he said. "Once you know that, you can widen the investigation."

"But I'm grounded. How —?"

"Go to your window. What do you see?"

Confused, I got up and parted the blinds. "Chantelle," I whispered. She was on the scooter, holding the floral helmet in her hand.

"She will take you to where you need to be," Klimt said.

While Mom and Josie were out of the way. A shiver of excitement thrust its way into my thumping heart.

"Good-bye, Michael. No more help."

"Mr. Klimt, wait."

But the phone clicked off.

And I was on my own.

Once again we headed out toward the coast, going as far as Coxborough village before Chantelle turned us toward the sea and an isolated row of gray stone cottages. There were four in a terrace that had once been owned by local fisher-men. Judging by the cars that were outside now, none of these people fished for a living.

Chantelle stopped by the first cottage in the row. It was prettier than the rest and still had the old wooden shutters at the windows, plus a white picket fence to match. A sign near the front door named the house RESTFUL. Wallflowers were growing up all around it.

"Are you going to sit there all morning, Michael?"

The scooter's engine was quietly humming.

"You're leaving me here?"

"I will be back in one hour. If you're not outside, waiting, you will walk home, okay? It would be wise to remember that your mother sometimes returns for her lunch."

And if I wasn't at home studying . . .

Je comprend.

I got off the bike and unclipped my helmet, fixing it onto the back of the scooter. "Who lives here?"

"The people who own the dog."

"How do you know?"

"The police returned the dog to this address. It was not difficult to find this out."

This was a dig at my incompetence. The annoying thing was, she was right. I ought to have gotten this far by myself. All it would have taken was a call to the police with a general query about the dog's welfare. Any decent agent could have worked that out.

"What's their name?"

"Nolan. Dr. and Mrs. Nolan. One hour, Michael. Tick-tock. *Au revoir.*"

By now, the early morning haze had lifted and it was a beautiful, bright spring morning. The backdrop to the house was a blue, but not entirely cloudless, sky. I could feel the sun warming the back of my neck as I unlatched the gate and stepped onto the path. Right away, I heard sounds of a dog. Not a barking dog but a whining one, the noise Trace had made when I caught her on the cliff.

There was no bell, just a knocker in the shape of a fishing trawler. I rapped it gently. There were sounds of shooing and a door being closed.

Then the front door opened. Before me stood a slim woman, a bit older than Mom and starkly pretty around the eyes. Her fine black hair was swept off her face, clipped at the back so it fanned out behind her neck and shoulders. Apart from a pair of fluffy white slippers that frothed up over the ankles of her jeans, she was dressed like a woman having coffee with a friend. Earrings like the first true icicles of Christmas, patterned silk scarf, frilly white top, leather-link belt. Moneyed. Classy.

"Can I help you?" she said. She had a kind, well-educated voice.

"I hope so," I replied, trying not to look too casual, or nerdy. "My name's Michael. I —"

"Hang on. Aren't you the boy who . . . ? Yes, I recognize you from your picture in the paper."

Things could have gone either way at that point. I wasn't sure how she was taking this, though she had no real reason to dislike me. So I said very quickly, "I just wanted to make sure Trace was all right."

She smiled appreciatively, looking me up and down as if she were casting a part in a movie. "Would you like to come in? Trace is right inside. You can renew your acquaintance with her, if you like?"

I nodded. "Thanks. That would be cool."

I followed her into an open room. The whole interior had

a kind of soft beige glow, interrupted only by a gray stone fireplace and an upright piano along one wall. Unlike our house, the seats all seemed to have an acre of space around them, which was weird since the cottage looked small from the outside. It had been extended at the back into a sun-filled conservatory with sweeping views of the sea. A wide table occupied most of the conservatory. On the table was a newspaper, open at a crossword, next to what looked like a couple of science books. Beside the paper was a seagull-themed coffee cup, an ashtray with a cigarette still weeping smoke, and a bright pink laptop.

"Have a seat." Mrs. Nolan pointed to the conservatory chairs. I chose one next to a bookcase studded with books and family photos. On top of the unit was a sculpture of a dragon, a fire-spitting purple thing, encrusted with green and golden scales. "Don't mind that," she said. "We like dragons in this house — well, one of us does." She stubbed out the cigarette and closed the laptop. "I'll let Trace in. Be careful, she can be a bit frisky. Siberian huskies are something of a handful, but I suppose you know that now. We should have gotten something smaller, really, but Rafferty . . . Well, never mind. Would you like a glass of orange juice or something?"

"Do you have any soda?"

"Yes," she said brightly, and stepped into the kitchen. A

second or two later, I heard her saying, "Go on. Be good." And in came Trace, paws clattering on the wooden floor.

On the cliff, in the mist and rain, I hadn't been able to appreciate just how stunning a dog she was. Her thick, strong fur was a classic mix of black and white, with swabs of gray dabbed here and there. Her face and neck were purest white, topped by a deep ridge of black between her ears. A line of black drained out of the ridge, running from her forehead to the tip of her snout, dividing a pair of Nordic blue eyes. They in turn were lined by rims of black. It made me wonder if someone had invented mascara after studying the eyes of these amazing dogs.

She padded up to me and tilted her head, holding her crescent-shaped tail quite still. She was confused and a little suspicious. I felt hollow in my stomach. Maybe it wasn't such a great idea to be left alone with a large doggy wolf.

"It's okay," I whispered.

Her head tipped the other way.

And just as in the car when the police had stopped us, I began to get a strange impression of her thoughts. This time it was more a jumbled rush, with snatches of the cliff and the coast road at night and a sudden glare of lights and . . .

Just then, Trace began to howl, as if she'd heard a noise at a frequency only a dog could detect. At the same time, the bookcase creaked and a framed photograph fell over, making me jump. Mrs. Nolan was in the kitchen doorway, staring, pale-faced, at the shelves.

She dropped my glass of soda on the floor.

We both stared at the epicenter of the explosion, at the crown of splattered cola seeping under the baseboards. Then she got herself together and hurried for a cloth. By the time she'd come back, I was down on my knees, picking up fragments of sticky glass. I apologized, though I had done nothing wrong, and asked if she wanted me to leave. She said no, it was nothing, just a silly moment. But when I got up and righted the photograph, I could tell from the lost expression in her eyes that it was anything but a silly moment.

"Who is she?" I asked. In the frame was a picture of Trace as a puppy, being hugged by a teenage girl.

"My daughter, Rafferty," Mrs. Nolan said. The words floated out of her mouth like a boat slowly detaching from its moorings.

"She's very pretty."

"Thank you," she breathed. "She'd have liked hearing that. She was very self-conscious about her appearance."

I couldn't think why. She had striking eyes, just like her mother. "She looks —" *like you*, I was going to say, but Mrs. Nolan cut me off in spectacular style.

"She died, just over three years ago. An accident. Here on Berry Head."

I picked up the photo again. A beautiful girl and her happy dog, frozen in a wooden rectangle of time. Trace, who'd been sniffing at the cola spill, jumped onto a sofa in the living room and flopped down.

"What happened?"

"She was cycling home from the village one night when she fell off her bike. She'd been warned many times about riding too fast, in the dark, but she was young and . . ." Mrs. Nolan passed the wet cloth from one hand to the other. "Her head struck a rock and she was knocked unconscious. She bled, very badly. She lay in the road for some time, we think, before she was found by a passing motorist. He called an ambulance. They rushed her into Holton. She died shortly after being admitted."

"That's terrible."

"Yes. Worse than terrible. You can't imagine what it's like to have someone you love so dearly plucked out of your life for no apparent reason."

That, of course, made me think about Dad. And my own grief must have been as wide as the sea, because Mrs. Nolan immediately said, "Oh, I'm sorry. That was a horrible, selfish thing to say. Please forgive me. Have you lost someone, too?"

"My dad," I said quietly. "He ... went away and never came back." I put the photograph back on the shelf.

"Oh, not there." She reached out a hand. "Next to the music award, if you would."

There were several silver cups along the shelf, all decorated with golfing badges. Nearest me was a smaller trophy — a music stand planted in a block of wood. On the stand, where the sheets of music would have been, was an inscription. I didn't read it, but Mrs. Nolan said, "Rafferty was very musical."

I nodded and looked at the piano.

"Do you play?"

"No."

Mrs. Nolan hit a key. The note circled around the living room, making Trace prick her ears. "She was coming home from a piano lesson that night. No one's ever played this instrument since. Liam says we ought to get rid of it, but I can't, not yet."

"Liam?" I said.

"My husband," she replied. "He's not a sentimental man." She smiled sadly and looked at the photograph. "I'll get you another glass of soda."

When she came back in, I was sitting at the table, reading the spines of her books. They had weird titles like *Synastry in the Aquarian Age* and *Parts of Fortune, Paths of Love.*

"Astrology," she explained. "I draw up charts for people. You're an Aries, aren't you?"

"Um, yes," I answered. In fact, it was my birthday in a couple of weeks' time. "How did you know?"

"It's those eyes. They're full of gentle determination. A word of advice, Michael. Life should be a joy, not a string of challenges."

I smiled politely, trying to "read" her like my dad might have done. I thought I felt a kind of glow coming off her, as if she'd been dipped into a soothing orange flame. After a second, when I still hadn't spoken, she raised an eyebrow to prompt a response. I smiled again and decided to press on. At the moment, my life was all about challenges; I still had a UNICORNE file to solve. "Mrs. Nolan, can I ask you a question?"

"Call me Aileen, please." She handed me the fresh glass of soda. I took a sip and put it down on the paper, careful to avoid the unfinished crossword.

"The journalist who wrote about me catching Trace told me she belonged to someone else — a girl at my school. Why would she say that?"

"If it's the girl I'm thinking of," Aileen said, finding a coaster to put under my glass, "a slightly scruffy type who likes to hug the coastline and stare at the sea . . . ?"

I nodded. That sounded like Freya.

". . . Trace has been seen with her several times. The reporters must have talked to someone who assumed they were connected. Odd, though. We've lived on this coast for nearly nine years and there aren't that many houses close by. I thought everyone here knew Trace was ours."

She shrugged and went on, "That day you caught her isn't the first time she's been loose. A couple of months ago, Liam was walking her when Trace became agitated and took off toward one of the old World War Two defense shelters. The girl was inside. By the time Liam got there, Trace was jumping up, nuzzling her, doing what dogs do. The girl was a bit overwhelmed, he said, but didn't seem to mind too much. She even told him she liked huskies, though she'd never been much of a dog lover generally — which showed in the way she petted her, Liam said."

"How do you mean?"

Aileen pulled out a chair and sat down. "Most people ruffle a dog's fur or scratch behind its ears. The girl ran her fingers over Trace's head like a blind person feeling the shape of an object. Then she drew back quickly and asked Liam to leave. Liam didn't like her attitude much; he doesn't tolerate rudeness in children very well. But when he tried to pull Trace away, she dug in her claws and almost bit him. The girl ran from the shelter. That's when the trouble really began. Trace broke free and chased after her. Liam caught up and put Trace on the leash, but he had to whip her to stop her howling."

"Whip her?" I hadn't even met Liam Nolan and already I had a deep dislike of him.

Aileen chewed her lip. "She hasn't been the same dog since. I've had her checked, but the vet can find nothing wrong. We really don't know what's upsetting her."

I glanced at Trace, who was calm enough now. She had settled in with her snout between her paws. Her bright blue eyes were open, staring, as if she were pondering her next escape. "Have you spoken to Freya — that's the girl's name — to ask why Trace might have run to her?"

Aileen turned to the window and peered for a while at the distant horizon. "A week later, the same thing happened. This time, the girl became very distressed. Liam did his best to calm her down, but she virtually accused him of stalking her. When we walk Trace now, we have to keep her on the leash. If we don't, she bolts toward the village. Don't ask me how she did it, but she found the girl's house. She's been there twice. The last time Liam went to retrieve her, he was forced into a confrontation with the girl's father. It's difficult to know what to do. I daren't even let Trace loose in the garden. A ten-foot gate couldn't keep her in. The morning you caught her, I'd let her out to do her business — and suddenly she was gone, just a blur in the rain. We're tired of trying to work out what's gotten into her. I probably shouldn't say this, but we're considering giving her to a dog shelter, somewhere well away from here."

"You can't do that," I said.

She looked at me with a compassionate smile. "It's harsh on Trace, I know, but . . ."

"Wouldn't Rafferty have wanted you to keep her?"

That touched a nerve. She found a pack of cigarettes, shuffled one out and then thought better of it. "Bad habit," she said. She tossed the pack aside. "You're an interesting young man, Michael. Quite thoughtful for your age. Why aren't you in school, by the way?"

Luckily, I had an answer for that. "Um, I had a sinus infection and had to take some pills. I'm better now, but

Mom says I have to finish out the prescription and she's worried that —"

"You'll forget to take your pills at school?"

"Or lose them." Like Josie had once.

Aileen smiled at the photograph of Rafferty. "The trials of being a mother."

Quite.

She stood up and walked to the window, picking up a tiny watering can. "This Freya girl, how well do you know her?"

"She's in my class."

"Oh?" She held the can aside. "You know her quite well, then?"

"Not really. She's new. She's a bit of a loner."

"Well, yes. That figures. But a classmate all the same?"

"Hmm." I nodded.

She tended a potted plant on the far end of the table, nipping off dead leaves before she watered it. "Is it possible you could speak to her for us?"

I took a drink of soda and made it last. "I could try — but I don't think it would stop Trace looking for her."

"No, perhaps not." She put down the watering can. "It's not fair to drag you into it, anyway."

But I wanted to help her. I really did. Out of nowhere,

I heard myself saying, "I could take Trace out for a walk, if you like?"

Aileen's dark eyes widened in surprise.

"If Freya saw her with someone she knows, then . . ."

I wasn't sure where I was going with this, but I could see Aileen's thoughts whirring as she stared into the middle distance of the living room. In an instant, she'd reached a decision. "Are you in a rush?"

"Sorry?"

"Do you have to be somewhere in the next half hour?"

I glanced at my watch, ever wary of Chantelle's warning. Twenty-five minutes had already slipped by. "No," I said, a little uncertainly.

"Then why don't we walk Trace now?" She went to the kitchen. At the rattle of the leash, Trace was off the sofa with her ears fully pricked.

Aileen clipped the leash to the end of a choke chain. "A note of caution, Michael: Huskies are incredibly strong. She weighs the better part of forty pounds and will take your arms out of the sockets if you let her. Don't be afraid to show her who's boss. They were used as sled dogs in the Arctic. Their handlers beat them if they got unruly." She crouched down and ruffled Trace's fur. "Yes, madam, I'm talking about you."

I looked at the dog. Well fed. Muscular. I wouldn't have bet on my chances in a fight.

Aileen reached into the hall for a jacket. "It's a great idea to let you walk her. We'll take her to the coast, well away from the village. You can hold her and get to know how she pulls. How does that sound?"

Apart from the fact that Mom would disown me if she knew what I was doing, it felt really neat to pick up that leash. "Ace," I said.

Aileen pulled on a woolly hat. "Excellent. Let's get some sea air."

She wasn't wrong about huskies. My upper arm felt like taut elastic as I reined Trace back and forth to keep her at heel. Be firm with her, Aileen advised. I tried, but Trace was either deaf or immune. The dog was walking me, not the other way around. The moment we steered away from the houses, she plotted her own course toward the sea.

"She's heading for the shelters," Aileen said, though we couldn't quite see them yet. They were built into the humps and hollows of the headland and were visible only looking inland from the cliff.

"Shall we go there?"

"Do you think she's got wind of the girl?"

I shook my head. "Freya should be at school."

Should be.

So we let Trace lead us to the first of the buildings, a sturdy shell made of brick that had once been a lookout for an invasion by sea. There was nothing in it now, no guns or other relics, just a groaning wooden bench where people came to sit and lovers carved their names and smokers discarded their cigarette butts. I let Trace sniff around in the corners. There was nothing to find. Not even the ghost of Rafferty Nolan.

I was looking down at the compass settings carved into a worn gray flagstone by our feet, when Aileen said, "She watched sunsets from here."

"Rafferty?"

"Yes."

We both sat down, Aileen in a huddle with her hands in her pockets, nibbling the zipper of her designer jacket. It was cold in the shelter, out of the sun. I wrapped Trace's leash several times around my wrist, but the dog seemed content now to sit and pant. "Aileen, can I ask you something? When I caught her that morning, where on the coastline was she, do you know?"

She moved her gaze sideways toward me. "Don't you?"

"It was misty. I wasn't really paying attention."

"Well, you should have been. You picked her up near the landslide site." She nodded eastward. "There's been some erosion lately. One or two rockfalls. You didn't see the warning signs?"

"No."

"Good grief, your poor mother. Bad enough your running to the edge of the cliff, but to pick the most dangerous area as well? No wonder they said you're superhuman." She patted my arm and gave it a squeeze. "It was a very brave thing you did, Michael, and thank you, officially, for rescuing our dog, but let the police handle it next time, okay?"

A young gull, still brown in its feathers, toddled by, calling out for its mother. Trace rumbled, deep in her throat.

"Light snack," said Aileen, making me laugh.

I reached out and stroked the dog's black-and-white head. "Why did Trace go there?"

"To the landslide?"

"Yes."

"I have absolutely no idea. As I said, she's not been herself lately."

"Do you mind if we go and look?"

She pulled in her shoulders and shuddered. "Well, I admit I'd be happier back in the sun, but should we really be going up there?"

"I only want to see it. I just . . ."

"Boy thing. I know. I had four brothers, all of them crazy. Aries, I'm telling you, ruled by Mars. That daredevil streak is in your stars, young man. Do you like roller coasters?"

"No, not really." I'd been sick on one once, in Josie's lap. She'd refused to go to amusement parks with me ever since.

"Rafferty did. She used to scare us rigid with her extreme

rides and bungee jumps. She was keen to do a parachute leap. Would you like doing that?"

"I don't like heights."

She smiled and tapped my knee. "Says the boy who wants to go lurking near the cliff. All right. Keep a tight hold of Trace."

She jumped up smartly and Trace did the same, practically yanking me off the bench.

As we walked, the sun dipped behind a cloud. Trace was much calmer now and not treating me like an Inuit sled. Aileen said, "You're doing well with her."

"She's cool. I really like her."

"Good. I'm glad." We walked in silence for a few more steps. Then she said, "Can I ask you something? It's rather personal."

I shrugged and said, "Yes. Sure."

"You said your father went away a few years ago. Are you the son of Thomas Malone, the salesman who disappeared abroad?"

I looked down at my feet. "You know about it, then?"

"Only what I remember from the papers. I don't suppose there has been any news?"

And I had to answer no. Yet here she was, maybe part of the puzzle.

"I'd love to see his astrological chart," she said.

A cold shiver ran around my neck. I thought I heard my name being squealed on the wind and was so shocked I almost let go of Trace.

"Michael? Are you okay?"

"Yes," I said quickly. I tightened the leash and pulled Trace back. I looked at Aileen and nodded. "Yes."

"I'm sorry," she sighed. "I shouldn't have said that. I wouldn't want you to think you could use astrology to predict what might have happened to your father."

"It's okay. I understand." So why did I feel like my hopes had been dashed? "Why would you want to see his chart, anyway?"

She moved a wisp of hair from across her lips. "Oh, I don't know. Curiosity, I suppose. It's what astrologers do. We look at the charts of our loved ones first, then move on to the planets of historical figures, then we start applying what insights we've gained to the people around us, trying to figure out what makes them tick. It's not an exact science. Most of it's done by instinct, to be honest."

"Have you looked at Rafferty's chart?"

"Oh, yes, many times. She mirrored her aspects beautifully, Rafferty did. So much Neptune in that girl's chart."

"What does that mean?"

"Artistic. Spiritual. Highly imaginative. She was drawn

to all things mystical. Dragons. UFOs. Reincarnation. She and Liam were always arguing about it. He's a down-to-earth, practical man who believes the world is what it is, and nothing more. He wanted Rafferty to follow him into the medical profession, but all she ever talked about was running a chain of health food shops and living in Paris, drawing portraits of old ladies."

"Old ladies?"

Aileen laughed and shook her hair back over her shoulders. "She liked their faces. She was a talented artist as well as a promising musician. Sorry, I'm sounding like the awful mother on parents' night who can't stop boasting about her little princess."

"It's okay."

She patted my arm. "Thank you, whether you meant it or not." She pointed directly ahead. "There."

In the distance was a bright red DANGER sign, wavering gently in the breeze. The area had not been cordoned off, but other walkers were staying well clear of it. "Will you hold Trace for me? I want to go nearer."

"I'm not sure that's a good idea," she said.

I slipped the leash off my wrist. "There must be a reason why Trace was here that morning. I just want to get a closer look. If I stand on that ridge, I can see down, okay?" I pointed at a grassy hump some ten yards back from the edge.

"Promise me you won't do anything silly."

"Promise," I said, and handed her the dog.

I ran up the ridge, only slowing when I heard Aileen shouting, *"Be careful!"* I looked back and raised a hand in acknowledgment.

I mounted the ridge and looked over the cliff. It was one of those areas that didn't fall sheer to the rocks on the beach below but swelled out into a thick nub of land, dotted with a few bits of vegetation. I could see where part of the cliffside had collapsed, leaving a mound of sandstone rubble shoring up the frothing sea. Some twenty feet down was an old viewing platform, bound by rusted railings. The steps to it were overgrown with lichens and moss, but a few were still visible through the scrub. Before the rockfall, it would have been safe to access. Now it was gated off with many more signs. And that's when a small truth came to me. Suddenly, I knew why Trace had been here. She wasn't going to jump off the cliff at all; she was going to jump the gate to the viewing platform — because someone must have been down there that morning. . . .

Suddenly, my breathing quickened and I seemed to have a minor reality shift. The sky grew unnaturally dark and a shower of fine rain closed in around me. From the fingers of creeping mist, my mind made a figure on the viewing platform. A girl with dark hair and milk-white hands, look-ing down at the killing sea.

"Rafferty . . ." I whispered.

The figure turned.

There was blood congealing from a wound to her temple, sticking her hair to the side of her face. But that wasn't what made my stomach lurch. As she turned around fully, she reached out and I saw her clearly.

It wasn't the girl in the picture in the house.

It was Freya Zielinski.

13 · DEAL

I told Aileen there was nothing at the landslide site, no clues as to why Trace should have been there.

"What were you hoping to find?" she asked. She looked back at the barriers and then again at me.

"I don't know. But there was nothing. Just . . . rocks and weeds." I shrugged and took hold of Trace's leash.

We walked away in silence, the wind at our backs. A couple of times Aileen glanced my way, but we were almost at the cottages before she spoke. "You like her, don't you?"

"Who, Trace?"

"Trace, yes — but I meant Freya."

I reeled Trace in and handed her over. "How did you know I was thinking about Freya?"

"Mother's instinct," she said with a smile. She held Trace close, patting the dog's neck. "Rafferty would have liked you, Michael. She always favored thoughtful boys."

I nodded, unsure of what to say. My head was still on that viewing platform. I couldn't put aside the horrible thought that Freya had been facing the sea that morning, ready to throw herself into the water. What could drive a girl her age to want to commit such a dreadful act? I looked at Aileen, who was still expecting a response to her statement. "Did Rafferty have a boyfriend?"

She laughed at that. "One or two. They never lasted long."

"Why? She sounds nice."

She smiled and traced a circle on the ground with her toe. "You've never been introduced to a girl's parents, have you?"

I shook my head.

"Well, when the time comes, remember this advice: Fathers are very protective of their daughters."

"You mean Liam scared them off?"

"Doused them in flame and blew their ashes across the sea would be a more accurate description. Rafferty didn't live long enough to really enjoy the company of boys, but very few would have gotten past Liam."

I stood up straight. "I wish I could have met her."

"Me, too," Aileen said. "Me, too. I miss her terribly, as I'm sure you miss your father. But we're healing slowly, even Trace." She squeezed the dog's ear. "At least some good did come from her death. I can always take comfort from that."

"Some good?" I asked.

But she'd turned her head toward the road. "Do you know that young woman?"

I heard the thrum of a scooter engine.

Oh, heck! The time!

Chantelle was there with the motor running, keeping the scooter steady with her feet. I was ninety seconds over the hour, and ticking. "Um, yes. She's come to pick me up — I hope."

"You hope?"

She didn't know Chantelle. I had visions of me getting within five yards of the scooter and her leaving me choking in a cloud of exhaust.

"She looks a bit impatient. You'd better hurry."

I took a hesitant step toward the road. "You said something just now."

"I did? What was that?"

"Something about Rafferty doing good when she died."

"Oh . . . I'll explain next time. You go."

But a "next time" might not be so easy to arrange. I shifted my balance back toward Aileen.

Chantelle thrummed the engine again.

Final warning. I had to leave. Now.

"I'll be in touch, I promise. I'll talk to Freya." I skipped away backward.

"Go," Aileen laughed, and waved me away.

I skidded down the last piece of grass to the bike.

Chantelle said, "You have fifteen seconds to clean your shoes."

I dug out a tissue and wiped off the mud. "Why are you always so mean to me?"

"You're late," she said. "I am being kind. What have you learned from the Nolan woman?"

"Not much. Her husband, Liam, is a brute, and I think Freya wants to kill herself."

"She told you this? The woman?"

"No, it's just a theory."

"And these things are connected?"

"I don't know — possibly."

"This is not progress. Klimt will not be pleased."

I put on the helmet, and climbed onto the scooter. "Klimt won't be giving up on me now. Something bad is spooking Freya. I'm gonna find out what it is, whether UNICORNE helps me or not. Will you take me to the *Holton Post*?"

"Why?"

"I want to talk to Candy Streetham — about a girl called Rafferty Nolan."

She bypassed Holton and took me straight home. Apparently, Mom had called her while I was out, wanting to know if I was behaving myself. Chantelle had covered for me but feared Mom might drop in at lunch to make sure. I realized then why Chantelle had waited. Her threat to make me walk was an idle one. If Mom had come home and found me AWOL,

Chantelle would have been in trouble as well. She would also have to answer to Klimt. Rock and a hard place, as people like to say. It was in her best interests to get me back swiftly.

As it happened, Mom didn't come home for lunch, but Chantelle still wouldn't grant my request. She said I needed to be sure that Candy would be free and got me the number of the paper instead.

"Arrange a meeting for tomorrow." She threw me the phone. "And get the timing right."

I dialed the number. "I could just talk to her."

"She will want to see you. They always do. Make sure it's in an open space."

The telephone clicked. A receptionist asked which extension I wanted. I gave her Candy's name. The receptionist said, "Putting you through." She was replaced by a tinny snatch of classical music. The phone clicked again and a man's voice said, "Newsroom."

"Can I speak to Candy, please?"

"Candy's not at her desk right now. Do you want to leave a message?"

I raised my eyes to Chantelle, who could hear the man's voice. "Will you tell her Michael called, Michael Malone. She knows who I am."

The man said, "Can I ask what it's about?"

Chantelle shook her head.

"I'd rather speak to Candy, if that's okay?"

"No problem," he said. "I'll leave a message for her. Can she get you on the number you're calling from?"

"Yes."

"Malone, you said?"

"Michael, yes. Is this Eddie I'm speaking to?"

For a moment, a dead weight settled in the air.

"Eddie's out on a job," said the voice. "I'll make sure Candy gets your message." The line clicked and the dial tone buzzed. There were no good-byes.

"Okay?" Chantelle asked.

I gave her the handset. "I think so, yeah. I get nervous on phones. I'm not very good with them."

"Then I suggest the Civil War instead." She dropped a heavy textbook in my lap.

Merci beaucoup, mademoiselle.

It was another two hours before Candy got in touch. I was on my own by then. Chewing a pencil. Restless. Mom was still at work and Chantelle had gone to fetch Josie from school.

"Michael," she breezed. I could almost smell the mouth-wash flowing down the line. "I've got a sticky note on my computer screen saying you're ready to talk to me. Rescued any more huskies lately?"

"No," I said flatly. And since she'd brought it up, "You got it wrong."

"Sorry? I got what wrong?"

"The husky wasn't Freya's. It belonged to a girl called Rafferty Nolan."

"Rafferty Nolan?" She recognized the name. "Are you sure?"

"I met her mother today. She showed me a picture of Rafferty with Trace."

"Rafferty Nolan," Candy repeated. "That's very odd."

"Is it? Why?"

"Eddie said he spoke to a guy who told him Trace belonged to Freya, but given what happened to the Nolan kid, you'd have thought he would have known whose dog it was."

Which was more or less what Aileen had said. "Do you know who Eddie spoke to?"

"Not offhand. But I could find out. Why?"

"Nothing. Just . . . wondered."

There was a three-second pause that seemed like hours. I felt rattled again and almost put the phone down. But she seemed to realize she might lose me and said, "You know about Rafferty, then? You know what happened to her?"

"Yes. Did you do a story?"

"No, but the paper did. I was a cub reporter at the time. They didn't let me loose on all the juicy stuff. Rafferty Nolan was headline news. Pretty girl. Tragic accident. Grieving parents. Her death kicked off a safety campaign warning kids about the dangers of riding bikes without adequate protection."

"Some good," I muttered, remembering what Aileen had said.

"There was a boom in the sale of cycling helmets, if that's what you mean. Anyway, that's Rafferty's story in a nutshell. Unless . . ."

"What?"

"You know something I don't?"

Another pause. More awkward than the first. Why did she make me feel so uncomfortable? I said quickly, "I want to read about Rafferty because I helped Trace." And because I was looking for any kind of link between Rafferty and Freya, though I wasn't going to tell the *Holton Post* that.

Candy made a puckering noise with her lips. "Okay, I'll do you a deal. I'll get you what I can on Rafferty Nolan as long as you talk about that day on the cliff."

"Deal," I said. "Where shall we meet?"

"I don't mind. What time d'you get out of school?"

"I'm suspended. I can see you at ten tomorrow morning."

"Suspended? What the heck did you do, wonder boy?"

"It's . . . complicated."

"Now, why doesn't that surprise me? Has this got anything to do with your interest in Rafferty?"

"Ten," I said. "At the shelter on Berry Head."

I spent the rest of that day pretending to work. I wanted to be sure that when Mom looked in, she'd approve of my room being untidy for once. We exchanged a few muted words, mainly about the essay I'd been "writing." When she left, she kissed the top of my head and said Josie could come in for ten minutes as a reward for my good behavior. I managed to remember to smile and say thank you. Half an hour later, Josie slipped in and arranged herself, pixie-style, on the bed. She was still in her uniform, minus her tie. She opened her bag and spilled some swag. She'd smuggled me a plate of cookies from the kitchen, plus a Mars bar, a comic, and my old iPod. Of less delight was her report on Freya.

"Saw her."

"And?"

"You know that spot by the science building where that kid got in trouble for skateboarding?"

"Josie, get to the point."

"She was on the wall there, at lunch. Me and Tirion went

and sat near her. Not close enough to cramp her style or anything, but near enough so she could hear us talking."

"Did you speak to her?"

"Michael, don't be dumb." She tossed her hair behind one ear. (What was it about that move that said *Boys, as a breed, will never understand us*?) "I'd gotten a dragon book out of the library and I pretended to show Tirion pictures from it, going, 'Aww, look at that one. Dragons are *so* cool. They make fire in their tonsils, you know.'"

"Tonsils? Dragons don't have *tonsils*."

She waved her hands in the air. "Well, obviously, duh. I was expecting her to butt in and say, 'No, they don't.' I was being clever."

"So what did she say?"

"Nothing. She sort of huffed, then got up and walked away."

"Josie, that's useless."

"Well, what was I supposed to do? I could hardly just barge in and start asking her to tell me her life story, could I? 'Hello, I'm Josie from Wikipedia. I'd like to know everything about you, please.' Anyway, so now I've tried your stupid dragon plan. Tomorrow, I'll tell her you want to go out with her."

"Eh? What? NO!"

"Look on the bright side. She might say yes."

"Exactly!"

"Don't flatter yourself, Michael. You're not *that* good-looking."

"Josie, watch my lips: Do NOT tell Freya I want to go out with her."

"Why not? She's bound to tell you everything you want to know, then. You don't wanna let Garvey beat you to it."

"Ryan? Why would Ryan want to be with Freya? He hates Freya."

"Oh, *Michael*."

"What?"

"You're so lame about girls. When a boy disses a girl as much as Ryan disses Freya, it means he secretly likes her. He just wants everyone to think she's gross before he moves in on her himself, right?"

"If you say so," I conceded weakly. Ryan and Freya? He'd have better luck in an alligator swamp. I made a mental note that when I got back to school, I would talk to Ryan about Freya. He was bound to dis her as Josie had said, which would make him the perfect guinea pig for testing this "flecking" thing Dad had perfected. I hadn't had a chance to try it yet. Maybe now, on Josie? I strengthened my gaze.

She immediately said, "Um, what are you doing?"

I lifted my shoulders. "Nothing. Just look at me."

"You're staring at my eyes. It's kinda gross, Michael."

"I thought I saw something."

"That would be your dazzling reflection," she said. "Stop it, will you? You're freaking me out."

"Just hold still and look at me," I tutted. I thought I could see some bright red flecks beginning to sparkle. The tiniest of tiny points of light. A sign of her growing annoyance, perhaps?

"Right," she huffed. "If you're going to act weird, I'm going downstairs."

"No, wait. I thought I saw a fly, that's all."

"No, you *didn't*," she said, screwing up her nose. "What's the matter with you? Stop messing around."

Definite red flecks. This was working. All I needed now was a positive test.

"Hey, Jose, do you love me?"

She sloped her gaze upward and I almost missed the change. "No," she said in a grumpy little voice. Like an asteroid belt around a dark planet, a whole ring of green dots flared for a moment. I knew, of course, that Josie was lying. And now I knew green was the color of it.

"Thanks," I said, grinning.

She scowled at me, hard. "Right. I'm gonna tell Mom that staying in your room too long is making you mental."

I raised my hands in surrender before she could jump off the bed. "Okay, I was being dumb. I'm sorry. Only sensible questions from now on, promise. Starting with . . . did you find out about Freya's operation?"

She held up her middle finger. For one moment, I thought she was telling me what she really thought of her not-so-handsome, slightly "mental" brother. Then I noticed the end of the finger was wrapped in a bandage. "I cut myself for you."

"Cut yourself? Why?"

She rolled her eyes. "Because it meant I'd get sent to the nurse, stupid. What do nurses know about?"

"Health records." Smart.

She clasped her hands and pitched her voice high. "Oh, thank goodness, my brother has a brain."

Yeah, very funny. I knew it had been a mistake for her to be cast as Dorothy in the school production of *The Wizard of Oz*. "What did she say — the nurse, I mean?"

"Nothing."

"Josie?!"

"She said she wasn't allowed to talk about other pupils and had I had my measles vaccination yet?"

I sank into my chair.

"I did *try*, Michael."

Big flash of gold. She was telling the truth.

"Josie, time's up!" Mom called from downstairs.

Josie made monster hands at the door. She shuffled

herself to the edge of the bed and put her arms around me. "I know you're up to something. Don't do anything dumb without telling me, will you?"

"Course not," I said. But my lips were sealed, and she left the room no wiser than when she'd entered.

I told Chantelle I had to meet Candy alone. I would cycle there, I said.

She wasn't happy. "Klimt's orders are for me to protect you."

From what? Ghosts? Goths? Overpowering mouthwash?

"It's just a meeting. I won't mention UNICORNE or Dad."

"I should follow you."

"What for? We're only going to talk."

"I'm supposed to look after you."

"Fine. I'll have a Coke and a bag of chips next time you come up."

She rolled out that Gallic scowl she was so good at. "I am not your — how do you say it? — maiden."

"I think the word you're looking for is *nursemaid*," I said.

She wafted a hand, crossed over to the window, and parted the blinds. She was wearing flat shoes and a plain green dress with a hemline just below the knee. "All right. You can see this journalist woman. But call me if you're in any kind of trouble. If you're not home by eleven, I will come to the shelter. Repeat what I said."

"You're not my maiden."

"Not *that* part."

"Home by eleven or call."

"Good. Put your phone on Record."

"Why?"

"Because I want to know what this journalist knows. This is standard practice for UNICORNE agents. We record *everything*. Just do it, okay?"

So I found the Record app on my phone and set it running from the moment I left the house. Now she could play the whole journey back: everything from opening the garage doors to riding to the shelter and quizzing Candy.

It was quiet on the headland, no walkers about. The wind was chasing in from the sea, tugging at my cap and whistling through the spokes of the bike. I had never been great on a bike and was pleased there was no one to see me wobble.

As I began to climb the hill, I couldn't help thinking about Rafferty Nolan and what conditions might have been like on the night she'd had her accident. Calm, perhaps, if she'd been pedaling fast. I told myself I wouldn't want to hurtle down this road. There were potholes everywhere, like mousetraps waiting to snap. Here and there I could see rough boulders and stones jutting out of the grassy shoulder. Which one, I wondered, did Rafferty haunt? Which of these blunt objects had found itself strewn with memorial flowers some three years ago?

My mind switched sideways to Freya. At the same time, I saw a car in the distance, one black speck in a thousand bits of trivia the eye takes in at every moment. I didn't think anything of it. Instead, I started going over what Josie had said. She was right (as usual). If I wanted sensitive information, there was no better way than to buddy up to Freya. But asking her out was surely not an option. For one thing, I'd never asked *any* girl out. And Freya wasn't just any girl. How scary would *that* be, having her bird's-nest hair on my shoulder? Or people seeing us holding hands in public? Or —?

Michael.

I heard a voice on the wind. My gaze flashed to the side of the road, where I thought I saw the wispy figure of a girl. But all I knew next was a wall of black. The car was in front of me. A roaring noise of tires and hot metal. There was no dividing line down the road and very little room for more than one vehicle. I didn't know whether I had wobbled toward the car or it had veered toward me. But in that instant, I knew how a seagull feels when it ventures into the middle of the highway, hoping to snatch a piece of roadkill. The skillful birds know when to fly, until the day they meet the driver who floors the pedal.

There was an impact — of sorts. I heard my bike wheels crumple and grind along the road.

The car and its death thrust passed underneath me.

And I was flying upward, but not like a gull.

I immediately knew it had happened again. That I'd messed with time and changed my reality. But this experience was different from the others. I'd had no chance to think about it, no time to imagine where I wanted to be or the best means to escape a collision. My brain just entered survival mode. For a nanosecond I was in the air, out of my body, hovering, safe. Then I plummeted down, missing the car and landing with a BANG on the potholed road. Then there was stillness, a peace that seemed to last for a thousand years. Until I felt a cool hand pressing on my head and a soft voice whispering, "Michael, come back. . . ."

"Rafferty . . ." I whispered. And the hand fell away.

And then I woke up.

And there was Chantelle . . .

. . . In a uniform, a light blue nurse's uniform.

"Where am I?" I said. My mouth felt drier than a parched salt lake. I tried to sit up, but every muscle from my shoulder blades up was on fire. I fell back against a stack of pillows, trying to spit a plastic tube from my mouth.

"Easy, easy," Chantelle said, supporting my head and at the same time calling, "Darcy! He's awake!" as if I were a monster on Frankenstein's slab. Feeling trickled back into my arms and legs, and it genuinely felt as if ten thousand volts of electrical charge had passed through my body.

It lives! But it *hurts.*

"Oh my God, Michael! Oh my God! Oh my God!" Mom came rushing in, skidding like a kitten chasing paper across a slippery floor. She was wearing her outdoor coat and scarf. She clamped my hand (which hurt like crazy) and lifted it to her trembling lips.

"Nice and steady," said Chantelle, removing the tube. "He's very weak."

"You're . . . a nurse," I whispered.

"Of course I am," she said.

"Chantelle has been looking after you," said Mom, "while you've been . . ." She squeezed my hand harder.

Ow! Moth-err.

I was in a hospital room. I could see that now. One chair. A small cart with some dressings and meds. A nightstand with a sprinkling of get-well cards. On the far wall was a small TV. Above the bed, a row of halogen lights was fighting to repel the daytime sun that was slanting in through an open window. In the space beside the window was a painting of a fishing boat. On the masthead of the boat, a gull was perched.

Roadkill.

"The car . . ." I said. It all came back in a horrible flash.

"Not now," said Chantelle, lifting me a little and plumping the pillows. "You need to rest." Across the bed, she said quietly to Mom, "Keep him calm. I'll go and find one of the medics."

Despite the pain, I sat myself up a little straighter. "Mom?"

"Yes, sweetheart?" Her eyes were filling up. She looked at me as if I'd just been born.

"Is Chantelle . . . ?" I blinked and made sure she was out of the room.

"What?"

"Is she still . . . our au pair . . . ?"

There was a pause. Mom spluttered with laughter. "Goodness, that must have been some bang on the head. No, darling. Chantelle works here. She's been at your bedside all week."

"All *week*?" I'd been out for a *week*?

"Shush. You heard her. You're supposed to stay calm."

In the pain stakes, not a bad idea. I looked at my hands. One was wrapped in bandages. The other was plum-colored (all varieties), and some kind of plastic thing was taped to my wrist and seemed to be inserted into a vein. "I'm sorry, Mom."

"What for?" She looked puzzled.

"I shouldn't have gone out. I should have stayed in my room." I couldn't remember why, but I was pretty sure I'd broken some sort of curfew.

But Mom didn't seem to see it like that. Leaning forward, she pushed my hair from my eyes. "You were perfectly entitled to go and meet your friend."

"Friend? What friend?"

"Slow down," she said. "Don't tax your brain. When Josie gets here, she'll want to claim exclusive rights to that." She stroked my brow, a little longer than she needed to. "The police want to talk to you."

"Why? What have I done?"

"Nothing." She laughed. "You've done nothing wrong.

They just . . . well, when something like this happens, they need to ask some questions."

Chantelle swept in again. "Sorry, no one is available at the moment, but a doctor will come in and see him shortly."

"I'll stay with him," said Mom. "I'll call Josie and tell her I'll be late."

"He'll be perfectly all right with me," said Chantelle. "You go if you need to. He can watch TV while we run some checks on him."

"Well . . ." Mom picked up her bag.

"Don't leave," I pleaded. I'd been dead to the world for a week. I wanted to know what was happening in my life. I wanted to actually *see* my mom.

Chantelle stepped forward and felt my pulse. "Hey, no jumping around. I don't want you disturbing this IV." She retightened the tape on the thing on my wrist.

Mom leaned over and gave me a kiss. "I'll be right back, with Josie. Better prepare yourself for an onslaught. She hasn't seen you since . . . this happened. Be good. Do exactly as Chantelle tells you."

"I'm hardly gonna party in here, am I?"

"Boys," Mom sighed. "You can knock the stuffing out of them but never the lip." She gestured to Chantelle, who followed her out.

Just beyond the doorway, I heard them whispering.

"He seems a bit confused. I'd like Dr. . . ." Kay, I thought Mom said. Dr. Kay to look at him.

"I'll arrange it," Chantelle reassured her. "He's off duty at the moment, but shall I . . ." something "him, for you?" Page him, maybe? "You'll need to be here when the police speak to Michael."

"Yes," Mom said.

And that was that.

Something like half an hour had passed before Mom came back. True to her word, Josie was with her. By then, the police were waiting in the corridor. Josie managed to pop her head into my room and wave like a frantic clockwork doll before being physically restrained by Mom. She was made to wait outside.

There were two of them, a man and a woman, detectives, both young and sharply dressed. They didn't look much like police at all. They asked me what I could remember of the accident. How fast did I think the car was going? Did it pass me and turn around? Did it seem to veer toward me? Did the driver lose control? Did I see the driver? Did the driver have anything in their hand? Could I describe the car? Make, model, color, license plate, any memorable or unusual features? Anything at all. No matter how small.

It was black, I told them. That was it.

They sat back, looking disappointed. The woman tapped her pen against her notepad. After what seemed like an age, she said, "Does the name Rafferty Nolan mean anything to you, Michael?"

The man glanced sideways at his colleague.

"I know that name from somewhere," said Mom.

"Please, let Michael answer," said the woman.

But the suddenness of the question had caught me unawares. I started doing that goldfish thing, where you're not quite sure what you want to say and your lips are moving but no words are coming out. I remembered the figure at the side of the road. Was that Rafferty, trying to warn me about the car?

The policewoman gave me another prompt. "Are you aware it was the Nolans' dog you rescued on the cliffs that morning?"

"Why are you asking him this?" said Mom.

The policewoman tightened her lips. She did that thing women sometimes do of dropping her shoe away from her heel. "Do you know the Nolan family, Michael? Is that where you were going — to the fishermen's cottages on Berry Head West?"

Mom said, "As far as I knew, he was going to see a friend."

I was?

"All the kids meet on the headland," she added.

The policewoman stared at me. My head felt like a strong-box she'd like to split open. "We talked to Michael's best friend, Ryan . . ."

"Garvey," the man filled in.

"He didn't say anything about a meeting that day."

Mom folded her arms. "Are you accusing Michael of lying?"

The policewoman cradled a smile on her mouth, the look of a woman who was getting nowhere. She stood up and circled around the back of her chair, sliding her notepad into her bag. "I was just trying to clarify why Michael was there, yards from the spot where a young girl lost her life three years ago, also in a bike-related incident. I find that an odd coincidence, don't you?"

"I don't believe in coincidence," Mom said.

"Me, neither," said the woman, buttoning her jacket. "We'll want to talk to you again, Michael, when you've had time to clear your thoughts."

She nodded at her colleague. And with that, they were gone.

"Well, I didn't like her attitude at all," Mom said.

"She is a cop," I said in the woman's defense.

"There's no harm in being polite." Mom fluffed her hair.

It was different, her hair. Darker. Less bobbed. I wasn't sure I liked it. "I'll let Josie in," Mom said.

"Mom, wait." I took her arm. "Why did they ask so much about the car?"

She paused and rested her hand on mine. "Whoever knocked you down didn't stop to help you. They were probably too afraid of the consequences. That's why the police are being prickly, I suppose. Someone from a cottage up the road heard the bang and called an ambulance."

"Aileen — Mrs. Nolan?"

"No, a man. He — So you *do* know the Nolan family?"

"I . . ."

Luckily, Josie spared me an explanation. She came in carrying a bunch of flowers. She slapped them on the bed by my ankles. "Hi! Oh, sorry. Those are for you. Freesias. Your favorite — so Mom says. I thought you hated flowers, but what do I know? We were going to bring grapes, but they had none in the store. *Wicked* bruise."

She was gawking at my eye.

"Oh, for goodness' sake," Mom tutted.

I hadn't seen my face yet. "Is it bad?"

"Mega."

"Josie, you're supposed to be making him feel better."

But I *was* feeling better. Josie mouthing off, Mom clucking like a hen. Normal. This was exactly what I needed.

Josie said, "You were in the papers again."

"For all the wrong reasons," Mom muttered. She picked up the flowers, looking around for a nonexistent vase.

Papers. Something swam into my consciousness about newspapers. That's why I was cycling on the headland that morning, to meet Candy Streetham, to talk about Rafferty. "Has Candy been around?"

Josie whipped her hair back and forth. "They sent a reporter, but it wasn't her. A man this time. He was *really* good-looking. Hey, they held a special assembly at school. Solomon said we had to pray for you! I saw Ryan, like this." She did a hands-clasped pose. "Ryan Garvey, *praying* — for you. Do you think he's gone soft?"

"Josie, that's enough." Mom whopped her with the flowers, spraying yellow petals all over the bed.

That made us all laugh.

"You sound better," said Chantelle, coming in with a glass of water and some pills. "Don't laugh too hard; there are stitches you don't know about yet." She pressed her fingers to a wound on my head. "Sit up further. You need to take these."

As I gulped the pills down, Josie started banging on some more about school. I wanted to hear it, if only to get some reference points for this latest shift, but her words started sounding like the sea in a shell as I focused instead on the conversation Mom and Chantelle were having. I picked out Mom saying, "Did you speak to Dr. Kay?"

Chantelle replied, "He'll see Michael later, after visiting is over."

They both looked at me and smiled. Smiles that said, *Yes, we're plotting, but it's in your best interests, dot, dot, dot.*

I was exhausted by the time Mom and Josie left, and ready to sleep again. But when Chantelle came in to close the blinds, I was surprised to hear I had another visitor. "She's been waiting for your mother and Josie to go. I've told her she can have a few minutes; that's all. I think she'd like to be alone with you."

Chantelle went out. Seconds later, a small bundle of gothic rags came in.

Freya.

She walked up and put a red rose on my chest. "Hi," she said in a squeaky little voice.

"Hi," I squeaked back. A rose? From Freya?

She stroked my bruised hand. "Look at you, all broken."

"I'm okay," I muttered. "Um, why are you here?"

She sighed and lifted her hand away. "I've come to steal your bandages for the school play. I've got the leading role in *The Mummy* this year."

"What?"

She tutted. "Why do you think I'm here?" She looked back at the door to check that no one was watching. "You're an idiot," she said. "You know that, don't you? But I guess that's always been part of your charm."

Then she bent over.

And kissed me, softly, on the tip of my nose.

As changes of reality went, this one was a real *wowzer*. That's, like, a zillion times greater than a *wow* and considerably weirder than a simple *er*. . . .

Kissed, by Freya Zielinski.

Where in my head had THAT come from?

"And she stuns him," she said as she straightened up.

She wasn't wrong. I'd practically corpsed. Flatline time on the heart rate monitor.

Beeeeeeeepppppppppp.

Followed by a sudden *KER-THUMP!*

It lives (again).

I gulped and slanted my eyes toward her.

"You can say something now, if you like," she said.

But nothing would come. My mouth and brain were still trying to process what had just happened.

She sighed and started to play with her bangles, rolling each one around her wrist in turn. "It was never like this in my fairy-tale books. You're supposed to wake up when the dark witch kisses you and forever be a handsome prince among men, riding away to far-off lands and slaying marauding dragons and stuff — except I'd finish with you if you did."

"*Finish* with me? *Ow.*" Reminder to self: Sudden movement *hurts*.

"Sorry. That would be very harsh. I shouldn't really give you too much grief, not when there's still a chance you might die."

"*What?*"

"Joke," she said, knuckling my arm. "You can't croak on me yet; I need you to get me through my history test. Nice pad, by the way."

Not from where I lay. "I don't like hospitals."

"*Excuse me?* More like private clinic. Your mom must be loaded. This place has got guards on the gate and everything." She made gun barrels with her fingers and sounded a double *kerpow.*

Was this real? Was this actually happening? Freya Zielinski doing . . . *girlfriend* stuff? I squeezed my eyes shut and opened them again. Yep, she was still there. Still a girl. Still a friend.

"Hey, you look good," she spoke up suddenly.

"Thanks, Freya, that's really funny."

"It was a prompt, Michael." She folded her arms. "Something *you* might say to *me?*"

Oh. Right.

Actually, she did look good. She'd made an effort, as Mom would say. She'd dabbed a little makeup around her eyes, painting the lids a light shade of green. And her hair was better. Still as wild as blackberry thorns, but not hiding her face anymore. She'd replaced her skull studs with silver stars and taken out the nose ring she wasn't supposed to wear at school but did. Bizarrely for her, she had a sweater on. A chunky-knit thing in royal blue with a single wave of white across the front.

Clocking where my eyes had rested, she said, "Present from my gran. I have to wear it. Some sort of family contract they make you sign at birth. Dad says I look like a Danish detective."

I frowned.

"I know. I didn't get it either."

"You look cool, Freya."

She curtsied. "Sire."

"I mean it."

"No, you don't."

"Yes, I do. You look . . ."

"Do not say 'nice.' I am never nice. Nice is not an option for vampires, Michael. Try 'I love the way your pale skin sparkles in the twilight.' I could just about cope with that."

"Don't make me laugh." I pointed to my stitches.

"Just these, in your head?" She ran her thumb along the area Chantelle had pressed.

"Careful! I think so, yeah."

"Only five? What a lightweight. On the stitches count, I rock."

And my head might have felt like a wrecking ball, but the brain inside was still in high gear. Here, at last, was my chance to quiz her about the elusive operation. "How many did you have, you know — for your . . . thing?"

She waggled my IV. Um, probably *not* a good idea, Freya.

"Only boys brag about their scars," she drawled. "Let's just say I won't be visiting any beach resorts ever."

"Is it really bad, then?"

She linked my little finger. "Really bad."

I couldn't believe it. Me and Freya, holding hands. And the weird thing was, it felt so right.

I liked her like this. Truly liked her. Smart, but not moody. Weird, but not wasted. Confident. Sassy. Different from the crowd. *Be careful what you wish for*, Klimt had said. How long had we been this friendly? I wondered.

She let go of my hand. Without prompting, she said, "I do like you, Michael, but I've had a heart broken once already. I'd need to be sure, really sure, before I let anyone get too close to this one. Is that fair?"

"Course," I said, though my brain was doing loops as it tried to unravel exactly what she'd said. She'd had surgery on her heart? At her age?

Wow.

That explained a lot about her vampire persona.

"Freya, can I ask you something?"

"If it's about the doughnut I bought on the way here, I ate it while they kept me waiting. Sorry."

"No. A serious question. Why did you call me an idiot when you came in the room?"

She gave me a look. "A ghost hunt? Come on."

"Sorry?" What the heck was she talking about?

"It was Garvey, wasn't it, who put it in your head?"

Put what in my head? "I can't remember."

She walked around to the other side of the bed. "After you were hit, he was mouthing off at school about some dead girl who's supposed to haunt the cliff." She lowered her voice to a pretty near perfect impression of Ryan. "'This is totally true, right. If you cycle along the coast road, you can see the dead girl sitting on the stone where she died. You can, like, talk to her and everything. If you put your hand through her, it comes back with her blood on it and you can't wash it off. Darren Egerton says if you make her mad, she comes after you with a bike chain, uh-huh, uh-huh, uh-huh.'"

"A bike chain?"

Freya shook her head in despair. "Garvey is a total jerk. He should be in a cage and have paying visitors. Anyway, I don't want to talk about this." She flapped her hands. "It freaks me out."

But I needed to tell her. She needed to know who the "dead girl" was. That Trace had belonged to her. That I'd met Aileen Nolan. That I'd probably seen Rafferty's ghost on the road.

"Freya —"

"You haven't gotten many cards, have you?" She was checking out the half dozen on the nightstand. "Did you like ours?" She held it up so I could see. A kid, like me, in a hospital bed, with his foot in bandages, winched up high. Inside, someone had written *Any Excuse to Get Out of Math!* and all my classmates had signed it. Freya stood it at the front of the group. "Can you believe that Lauren Shenton put two kisses below her name? I might have to seriously bite that girl."

I tried again. "Freya, there's something I need to tell you."

She pulled open the drawer of the nightstand. "Hey, there's another two cards in here."

Oh? There was room on the stand for several more cards. Why should two have been left in the drawer?

"They were underneath your med notes. Shall I read them to you?"

"Yeah," I said, a little confused.

"This one hasn't got an envelope." She showed me the picture. Two swans gliding across a pond. "'Dear Michael, I can't begin to tell you how shocked I was to hear what happened. Please, please get well. Come and see us when you do. Aileen N.' Who's that?"

Once again I tried to say, but Freya was on a crusade now. "What's it doing in a stupid drawer, anyway?" She plonked it onto the nightstand and slid the next card out of its envelope. She opened it and took out a folded piece of paper. Her eyes twitched as she read the sender's name. "Who's Candy?"

I only knew one. Candy Streetham. Candy Streetham had sent me a card? "She's a journalist. Let me see."

Instead, Freya unfolded the paper. It looked like some sort of photocopy.

"What is it?" I asked.

She took a sharp breath.

"Freya? What's the matter? What's on the paper?"

Her eyes skimmed it for about ten seconds. "How could you?" she said in a breathy whisper. "Not her. Anyone but her." She let the article drop to the floor.

"Freya?"

She backed away quickly, fingers fluttering against her temples.

"Chantelle!" I called out. "Something's wrong with Freya!"

And there was something very wrong in the room as well. A sudden gust of wind had swept through the window, billowing the blinds like a sail. My IV feed shook, the television flickered, the halogens blinked, the cart wheels skewed. Several petals were stripped off Freya's rose. At the same time, Candy's get-well card flew across the room and flattened itself against the wall. The piece of paper that had been enclosed with it spiraled through the air like bonfire ash. It landed on my bed within easy reach.

Freya screamed. She collided with the chair and tipped it over. Then she just ran, almost flooring Chantelle in her hurry to get out.

Shaking, I picked up the paper. On it was a picture of Rafferty Nolan, alongside an article about her accident.

"Michael, give me that." Chantelle was approaching with a hand stretched toward me. In the other, she held a gun. She was pointing it hard at the window.

Then a calm voice said, "Put the gun away, Chantelle. It would be useless, anyway."

And in walked Amadeus Klimt, wearing a white coat over his suit. On his lapel was a badge like Chantelle's. His simply said DR. K.

"Hello, Michael."

Chantelle raised the gun to ninety degrees, then buried it somewhere within her uniform.

"You," I said, panting slightly. "You're Dr. K." Or Kay, as my brain had interpreted it.

He righted the chair and picked up the card, dusting it before he dropped it on the bed. "People can find my name hard to pronounce."

"Like my mom, you mean?" I couldn't keep the unkind tone from my voice.

He spread his hands.

"You've met her, haven't you?"

"A delightful woman. Your father always thought himself a lucky man." He made a gesture to Chantelle to leave.

I watched her walk out of the room, but she was back within seconds, carrying a blue plastic tray. She put it on the cart and started rattling things around on it.

"What just happened?" I asked Klimt.

His gaze fell on the article. "Rafferty just happened. She has been around you for a while, I think."

"She's dead, Mr. Klimt."

He brushed a clear space on my top sheet, hitched his trousers, and perched on the bed, holding one ankle against his knee. "You disappoint me, Michael. What is death to a boy with your ability — surely just another form of reality?"

"Why was this in the drawer?" I flapped the article at him.

"Because we did not want your mother or sister to see it."

"And Freya?"

He tilted his head. The nucleus of one of his purple eyes sparkled as it caught the glare of the halogens. "That could have been avoided, but it is unimportant now."

"She was terrified. Where is she? Why did she run?"

Klimt picked up what was left of Freya's rose. He plucked the surviving petal, twisting it slowly in front of his face as if he could see every vein running through it. "Perhaps Freya knows more about Rafferty than she cares to admit. Read the article, Michael. It's time you learned how far your quest has brought you."

I looked at the picture of Rafferty Nolan. It was one of those standard high school shots. Head and shoulders, in her uniform. She was older here than in the picture at the house. A slightly gap-toothed, teenage girl. Wayward blond hair in natural ringlets. Lively eyes. Light, freckled skin. The camera loved her, as Candy might have said.

I read the headline. It told me nothing I didn't already know. LOCAL GIRL DIES IN TRAGIC ACCIDENT. But in the white space above it, in tiny blue scrawl, Candy had written a message:

Hey, kid. I hope you're feeling better by the time you read this. They tell me you're going to be okay, which is a relief. Thought I'd send you the info you wanted. This is from the Post *the day after the accident. It pretty much covers what happened to R. I talked to Eddie. He had nothing to add. But I did unearth two interesting facts. She was an artist, apparently, and always carried a small sketchbook with her. It disappeared that night and was never found. Also, one of the reporters who spoke to the mother found out the girl had an issue with her looks. You can't see it in the pic, but she had a birthmark on one side of her head. Her injury was on the other side, which would have seemed awfully cruel had she lived. Apart from that, she was a regular teen, good at school, liked by everyone. Get well soon. Godspeed, C.*

"A birthmark," I whispered, touching the picture.

Klimt nodded. "Are you closer to solving the puzzle now, Michael?"

Chantelle turned around. I was aware she might have something in her hands, but I was staring into the middle distance, remembering the fuss on the playing field and the mark I'd seen on Freya's head. "Is Rafferty . . . ?"

"Go on," he said. "Remember what we spoke about on

the cliff. The events most people consider ridiculous, UNICORNE treats as natural phenomena."

I tightened my gaze on Rafferty again. "Is she . . . living in Freya's body?"

"In a manner of speaking, yes. Rafferty Nolan carried one of these. Do you know what it is?" He held up an organ donor card. "Three years ago, Freya had an operation. She had her heart replaced."

"With *Rafferty's*?"

"Yes. I believe she's experiencing Rafferty's presence through a mechanism known as cellular memory, and you appear to be some sort of . . . catalyst for it." He swung off the bed, closing the blinds with a twist of his fingers. "I must congratulate you, Michael. You've done far better than I ever thought possible. I sent you out to solve the mystery of a stray dog and you've brought back evidence of a rare human condition. I had thought you too young to be of use to us yet, but it seems I've underestimated you. So we will proceed to the next level, a little earlier than anticipated." He nodded at Chantelle. She stepped up to the bed and quickly fed a needle into my IV.

"What's she doing?" I protested. But the drug was already in my system. I could feel my body going into slow motion. There would be no reality jumps on this occasion.

The room began to fall into a swirling hole. Klimt came

closer, weaving through my gaze like a watercolor figure. "Move him downstairs," he said to Chantelle. "Call me when his heartbeat has almost stopped."

"Whazz hap . . . ning?" I managed to say.

I felt Klimt pat my arm. "It's a little like dying, in a slow, controlled fashion. Relax, Michael. I'll see you on the other side."

"Hello, Michael."

I could hear Klimt's voice, but I couldn't see him. I couldn't even see myself. No hands, no feet, no visible body, just . . . the *essence* of me, floating over a never-ending whiteness. It was like looking through an aircraft window at a carpet of puffy clouds below.

"You can speak to me, Michael." His voice was detached, yet the sound waves were everywhere. "Just concentrate your thoughts, and your words will reach me."

"Where am I?"

"On a higher plane of consciousness. Do not be afraid. Nothing is going to hurt you."

"Why am I here?"

"For the single reason you've always been here — to find your father. The search begins now, with a small experiment."

"Experiment?" I said. There were no scientists in white coats or specimens in jars. And yet I had the strange impression that if I concentrated hard enough, I might create them from the clouds.

"Before you can begin to help us," said Klimt, "you must learn to control your reality shifts. So far, you have experienced a shift only during moments of emotional pressure. But if you are able to jump across the time lines at will, the multiverse becomes an open book."

A very BIG book. As far as I knew, our universe was infinite. And the multiverse sounded . . . bigger than that. It was one thing being able to travel across it, but you also had to know where you were going — didn't you?

Somewhere above me I heard a click, like the shutter of a camera lens opening and closing. As if he'd recorded my thoughts, Klimt said, "Theoretically, finding your father is simple. You merely replicate what you did on the cliff. Instead of waving good-bye on the morning Thomas left for New Mexico, you imagineer a scene where you are with him. In other words, you enter his time line exactly at the point he disappeared to you."

"But won't that mean I'll disappear as well?"

"Not if we train your mind carefully," Klimt said. "In this session, we will simply be assessing how capable you are of accepting suggestions. Follow my instructions and all will be well. You may detect some areas of pressure on your head. It will feel like someone is pressing their fingers against your skull. Do not be concerned. This is part of the procedure. Do you feel it?"

"Yes." It was exactly as he'd said. Two points of contact where my temples would be and another somewhere behind my left ear.

"I'm going to send you an image," he said. "A symbol, nothing more. It might take a moment."

I felt the pressure points intensify briefly, as if a small charge had been sent to an electrode. And then I saw what Klimt was sending. On a cloud up ahead stood a stunning black horse. An ebony mane was trailing down the side of its neck. A horn was spiraling out of its forehead. The moment I accepted it, it blinked an eye.

"Excellent," said Klimt. I heard the shutter sound again. "Go to it, Michael."

I was there almost as soon as I could think it. So close that it frightened me a little. The clouds seemed to shake and the image of the unicorn immediately turned fuzzy. I heard a whirring noise above me again and a voice much deeper than Klimt's said, "Stabilize him. Readjust the pressure."

Externally, I sensed a moving light. A tingle began in the corner of one eye and flared for a moment in the region of my neck. The unicorn shrank away from me, until our sizes were in the proportions of a normal boy and a horse.

Klimt said, "Good. You're doing well, Michael."

"Who's with you?" I asked him. "I heard a voice."

"A . . . colleague," he replied, after a pause. "Another friend of your father. Stay calm. Listen carefully. I want you to touch the unicorn now. All you have to do is imagine yourself stroking it. Can you try that for me?"

I raised an invisible hand. I let it rest on the unicorn's mane and felt the sensation of flowing hair.

"Good," said Klimt.

And the other voice said, "He's ready. Take him to the next level."

Klimt said, "Michael, this is important. I want you to think about your father now."

The moment I heard this, my world began to shake. A spiraling wind came out of nowhere and ripped at all my senses. The unicorn's body began to fragment as we entered some sort of escalating vortex. Pressure points popped all over my head like meteorites exploding on the surface of a planet. A new sound entered my consciousness. High-pitched, squeaking voices, gabbling in a language like nothing I'd ever heard. And although I couldn't tell what was being said, the mood was clear: They were exchanging notes of panic.

"Strengthen the imprint," the deep voice demanded.

And Klimt said urgently, "The unicorn, Michael. Keep your eyes on the unicorn."

There were more odd noises. Strobing lights. A sudden rush of heat all along one arm. But I did as Klimt instructed and looked for the horse. We were spinning rapidly, out of control. But some part of me remembered my mother telling Josie how to avoid dizziness when doing ballet turns: Focus, focus on a single point. I saw the unicorn's eye and held it steady. Gradually, the shaking and the spinning stopped and I was back, standing in front of it again.

There was a buzz and a kind of decelerating whir. I heard Klimt breathe a sigh of relief. "Well done, Michael. If that happens again, you know how to correct it. The black unicorn is your symbol of home. Place it firmly at the center of your mind and it will always bring you back to us."

A mauve light passed across my eyes, leaving behind an afterglow of purple. The contacts on my head had now doubled in number and were feeling more like clamps than fingertips. Klimt said, "We will try that again, but differently now. Can you think of an object — a gift, perhaps — that you always associate strongly with your father?"

Only one thing came to mind. I looked at the unicorn, and there around its neck was my paper chain of dragons.

"Perfect," said Klimt. The pressure points clustered in the center of my forehead. Whatever had been making the high-pitched squeaking noise now seemed to gurgle with pleasure. "Stay focused, Michael. The next step is crucial. I want you to take the dragons from the unicorn and attach them to yourself in some way. You may imagineer a suitable method as you wish."

As the pressure points tingled, I raised my nonexistent hand to stroke the unicorn's nose. It snorted and bucked, but remained stable. Reaching over its head, I took the paper chain off its neck, lifting it toward me, over the horn. But what had once been rough-cut paper was now a circle of fire-breathing creatures. They were purple, like the dragon in Rafferty's house, linked by a band of solid silver. I thought about Rafferty and how much she would like this: a crown of living dragons.

"Michael." Klimt's voice clicked in right away. "Do not let your imagination wander. Go back to the paper chain. Concentrate on the gift from your father."

"No," said the other voice, overruling Klimt. "Let's see where he goes with this. Tell him to put the crown on."

Then a third voice said, "Let me do it."

And with a sudden whoosh, Rafferty was standing where the unicorn had been, looking like her photograph in the paper. Green school uniform. Ringlets. Birthmark. Rafferty Nolan. Back from the dead.

A whole barrage of lights went off.

"Michael!" There was urgency in Amadeus Klimt. "Send Rafferty away. Go back to the unicorn."

But Rafferty's spirit was going nowhere. She put her hands around the crown. The dragons reared and puffed jets of smoke. "So cool," she said. "Kneel, I want to crown you."

I had the sensation of lowering myself.

"Michael!" Klimt's voice came louder and stronger. A huge impression of the black unicorn's head filled the space at Rafferty's back. She threw up a hand and made it disappear.

I felt her place the crown on my head.

"Get him back!" I heard the deep voice thunder. "How has the girl crossed the interface? Get him BACK!"

But Rafferty seemed to be stronger than they were.

She laughed and said boldly, "Arise, Michael, Lord of Dragons." And when I stood up, she took a pace forward and whispered in my ear, "Let's have a little fun."

With a whoop, she threw an arm around my neck and twisted me into her crazy world. The next thing I knew, I was flying down a log flume, carving up a runway of ice-cold water, about to hit another huge pool at the bottom. The moment the log went into the pool, the images switched and we were cresting the peak of a roller coaster track. Rafferty screamed as the car tipped forward and plunged us into a vertical descent before sweeping left on a gut-wrenching camber. I sensed it all, the steep rush of air, the g-force on my eyelids, the filth, the oil, the rick-rack of the track. I began to feel scared, really scared, like the way you do when you're inside a nightmare and you can't get out. All this time, I was aware that Klimt was trying to pull me clear. I could feel him in a tug-of-war with Rafferty's consciousness.

But he was losing.

I was out of control.

The "fun" continued, into its most extreme vision yet. The roller coaster leveled out onto a horizontal stretch of track, which then morphed into a stone bridge across a narrow river. In an instant, I was standing on the wall of the bridge, holding Rafferty's hand. For the first time, I noticed blood on her face, clawing its way from her temple to her neck. "Help me," she whispered. "Promise you'll help me and I'll let them have you back."

"What do you want me to do?"

Her green eyes narrowed. And in a voice like a wind from another world, she said, "Bring Freya to me."

"I promise," I replied.

And then we jumped.

The dragon crown tumbled toward the water. At first, the river was a dark gray slab. But with every frantic flap of my hands, it swelled into a raging torrent, foaming over rocks as sharp as talons. I screamed, certain I was going to die. Then I felt a powerful tug around my ankles and a cord pulled me back, and dropped me again and pulled me back, and dropped me and pulled me back, and . . .

. . . My eyes fluttered open. The bridge and the water and Rafferty were gone and I was in some kind of darkened laboratory, strapped to a table inside a glass pod. The pod was filled with a warm yellow fluid. I was immersed in the fluid and yet still breathing. Two pipes spouting from the pod were connected to a series of filters and pumps. Through the glass, I could see large banks of machinery. Small lights chasing other small lights. Lab technicians, flicking lights. Fixed above the pod on a semicircular track was a light shaped like a giant eye. Its outer edges were glowing mauve.

"Drain the tank," said the voice I'd heard beside Klimt's. "Erase all traces. Make sure he remembers nothing."

The pod jerked and began to tilt. As it lifted me upright, I saw a thickset man in a pin-striped suit step out of the lab through an unlit doorway. I didn't see his face. But across the room, in a pod identical to mine, I saw Amadeus Klimt. He was jerking, as if he'd had a massive shock. Suddenly, his head spilled violently sideways. Part of his hair had melted or burned. He gave another short spasm and an eye exploded from his head. I saw no blood, just a twist of wires. My heart rate tripled. But what I saw next really freaked me out. A creature not unlike a pale blue octopus crawled over Klimt's face and started to repair the damage to his eye, moving its tentacles like nothing I'd ever seen. My mind was just about coping with that when a similar creature appeared in front of me. I struggled against the clamps that were holding me. I screamed, but no sound came out of my mouth. The creature waggled a limb. From the end of the limb came a small, dark spike. I screamed as the creature put the spike inside my nose. A white light lit up the space behind my eyes.

And then I went blank.

My gran once told me that the first real sign of turning sea lion (I think she meant *senile*) is when you walk into a room to fetch something, but then you can't remember what you came in for. That was how I felt when I woke the next morning. I knew I had been on some kind of journey, but I couldn't remember a single detail. It was just as if someone had taken a brush and whitewashed a crucial part of my memory. It even took me several seconds to place Chantelle. As I stirred, she said, "Good sleep, Michael?"

I coughed and brought up something from my chest.

She was there in a moment, with a tissue, to catch my phlegm.

"My head hurts," I mumbled. And my nose, strangely. I placed a finger inside it and broke a slight crust of blood against my nail. "Ow, my nose is sore."

"You were dreaming," she said, tossing away the tissue, "throwing your head around in the night."

"Where am I?"

"In the clinic, where you've always been. We moved you to another room after . . . the incident."

A room with no window.

"Rafferty," I muttered. An image of me holding hands with her flashed through my mind but was gone so fast I couldn't trap it. A whole pile of other stuff rushed in instead. Rafferty's "visitation," Chantelle with a gun, Freya's heart transplant, Freya's *kiss*, her running away from my bedside in terror. "Where's Freya? I want to see Freya."

"You will, shortly," a familiar voice said.

In walked "Dr. K" in his usual immaculate suit, this time minus the doctor's coat.

"What's the matter, Michael? You look like you've seen a ghost."

Maybe I had. Somewhere not a zillion neurons away, I had the weirdest feeling that he ought to be dead. I even said, "You're . . . alive."

He smiled and wiggled his fingers for me. "I asked Chantelle to sedate you last night so we might carry out a small procedure. It's not uncommon to suffer some mild confusion. I hope your dreams were not too troubling."

"I don't remember my dreams," I said. My mind was always blank in the mornings — unlike Josie, who had colorful adventures every night. Our breakfast conversations were often dominated by her discoveries of pyramids on the moon or the strange things cows liked to talk about. But on this particular morning, I could feel my mind clawing at the edges of a dream. Falling. Water. Rafferty. A *promise*. Fragments, gone like dust in the wind. I looked at Chantelle and remembered her putting the needle in my arm. What was it Dr. K had said? Something about moving to the next level? "What have you done to me, Klimt?"

"*Mr.* Klimt," he said. He picked up a clipboard and flicked through some sheets of medical notes. "If you work for me, Michael, you will show me some respect. I take it he hasn't seen the mark yet?"

Chantelle shook her head. "I was waiting for you."

On a nod from him, she rolled back my covers. Oh, no. I was wearing my *Star Wars* pajamas. Chantelle had seen me in a pair of pj's with a Wookiee and a golden robot on the thigh. Someone take me out with a lightsaber. Now.

"Show him," said Klimt.

Chantelle raised my left leg off the bed and pushed the pajama halfway up my calf.

On my ankle, almost hidden in the shadows of my skin, was a small tattoo of a unicorn. It was UNICORNE's design, with the tail looped around itself, making an *e*.

"This confirms your recruitment," said Klimt. "You will not deliberately show it to anyone. If your mother or your sister should happen to see it, you must be prepared to say you paid for it and suffer any consequence arising from that. Congratulations, Michael. Welcome to UNICORNE."

Welcome to a year in my room, more like. "You could have told me what you were going to do. If Mom sees that, I am TOTALLY grounded. She hates tattoos. And what about my friends?"

"You undress before friends?"

"Um, *gym*?" I said. "Someone's bound to spot it. Then they'll all want a look."

Chantelle lowered my leg. "Say you had it done without your mother's consent. That will buy their secrecy and their respect."

Fair point. I smiled at Chantelle and she actually smiled back.

"The tattoo is not merely decorative," said Klimt. "It covers a microchip under your skin. The programming, in your case, was very advanced. We must be careful not to lose track of you, in case you have a sudden reality shift."

Tagged, like a dog. Was that a blessing or a curse? Either way, the unicorn did look cool. "I don't understand what I've done to deserve this. It wasn't me who found out about Rafferty's heart."

"But it was you who brought the case to our attention," he said. "And it's you who will continue the investigation when you leave. I want you to return to the Nolans' house — this time, taking Freya with you."

"*Freya?*"

Almost as soon as her name was spoken, Rafferty's voice swept through my mind. *Promise me . . .* it said. Like an oncoming train.

I gasped and covered my face.

"Michael?" Chantelle came up and parted my hands. "Michael, are you all right?"

"Yes, I . . . My head hurts a bit. Can I have a drink of water?"

Klimt stared at me a moment, then nodded his approval. While Chantelle was busy at the water cooler, I asked, "Why take Freya to Rafferty's house?"

"I am curious to see what happens," he said. "It should be clear to you now that Rafferty wants Freya to remember something, something that has kept her spirit from rest. Do you recall the hypothesis I mentioned yesterday?"

Chantelle came back with the water. The cold bite on my tongue almost made me spit. "Cellular something?"

"Cellular memory," he said. "A branch of our research has led to the suggestion that the physical donation of body parts can sometimes result in the transfer of the donor's memories. Imagine you received an organ from a Norwegian child and then discovered you could speak Norwegian or took a sudden interest in pine forests and fjords. That would be an example of cellular memory. There are many recorded instances of it, but none where the donor has returned to haunt the recipient. Freya is shutting Rafferty out because she does not understand what is happening to her. Your task when you leave here is simple. You will go to Freya and reassure her — and in doing so, find out what Rafferty knows."

"Are you going to . . . ?" What was that word people used about ghosts?

"Exorcise her spirit?" Klimt said.

That was it.

"We intend to help Rafferty . . . move on," he said. "But she has become of interest to us. Ghosts are not uncommon, of course, but they rarely form the kind of interstitial link that Rafferty has to you — or to Freya. We plan to study Rafferty's movements. It takes immense energy to cross the temporal interface and slip between the planes of human consciousness. We can learn from her. Forgive me, you seem puzzled. Should I make myself clearer?"

"Interface . . ." I muttered, pressing my temples. Why was that word sticking in my mind?

I leveled my gaze and thought I glimpsed a look of concern on Mr. Klimt's face. "Chantelle," he said quietly, "give Michael something for his headache, will you. A single dose of Meztamine should be sufficient."

She blinked her stunning brown eyes. "I'll have to go next door for that."

"Then go," he said, like a teacher dismissing an unruly child.

She threw a glance my way, then drifted from the room.

"What's Meztamine?" I said. It didn't sound like the sort of thing Mom might drop into her supermarket basket.

"A painkiller. It will calm your mind."

"I'm not anxious."

"As your doctor, I disagree." He fixed me with his purple-eyed stare. Was it my imagination or did his eyes look different? "You are about to return to the field, Michael. The thought of encountering Rafferty again must be making you slightly uncomfortable?"

"Not as bad as the thought of meeting Freya." I couldn't forget the words she had shouted just before she dropped the newspaper article: *How could you?* Those were the words of a girl betrayed. Making friends with her again might not be easy. "What if she doesn't want to know me anymore?"

"Then you must act like a UNICORNE agent, and use a little guile to renew her favor. You have more in common with Freya than you think. Cast your mind back to your early years. When you were young, you were very ill. So ill you almost died, did you not?"

"Yes. How —?" I stopped myself there. He probably knew what I ate for breakfast and how often I changed my socks. Downloading my medical history couldn't have been much of a challenge for him.

I was five when I'd had a rare form of leukemia. I'd only learned this from Mom the year after Dad disappeared. It was one of those things she'd only wanted to reveal when I was old enough to understand, she said.

My life in those days was an endless series of hospital visits, followed by years of dwindling checkups. What I didn't know, until Mom chose to spill, was that my chances of survival had been quite slim. She described how I'd lain in an intensive care unit, with nothing but tubes to the outside world. Four days of constant vigil, she'd said, when prayers were more important than sleep. Then the overwhelming relief when I began to pull through. She'd rambled for a while about guardian angels. And when I asked her, "Do angels really exist?" she'd replied, "I hope so, Michael. I really hope so. I pray there's one somewhere over New Mexico, looking out for your dad."

Mr. Klimt, who didn't strike me as an angel, said, "Your father saved your life by donating some of his bone marrow to you. It was fortunate for you that he was a match. Freya waited nine months for a suitable heart."

And she ended up with Rafferty Nolan's.

I pushed myself upright, causing a pillow to fall to the floor. "How long before I can leave?"

"Another day," said Chantelle, coming back into the room. She retrieved the pillow and stuffed it behind my shoulders. "No bones were broken in your accident, and your stitches were taken out while you slept. You can go home tomorrow. Here, take this." She handed me a pill in a small plastic cup.

"The police will call on you again," said Klimt. "Do not tell them you were going to meet Candy Streetham."

I looked at Chantelle, who'd obviously updated him. "We wiped your phone," she said.

"You don't think *Candy* was driving the car?"

"No, I do not," said Klimt. "But if the police believe you were going to meet a journalist, they will deepen their investigation. This is a case for UNICORNE now."

And I was an active part of it, a member of a secret organization that I still wasn't sure I could trust.

"The pill," he said.

I tipped it into my mouth and took a drink of water.

"Rest well, Michael. I will see you briefly tomorrow. You will keep us informed, through the usual channels." He nodded at Chantelle and started to leave.

"Wait. I want to ask you something."

He turned and looked at me, inviting the question. There

was definitely something wrong with his eyes. The left one appeared to be a slight shade of blue, yet I distinctly remembered that it used to be purple. "Did Dad have a unicorn on him?"

Klimt drew back and thought about this. "No," he said airily, twisting the ring on his little finger. "It was your father's disappearance that prompted us to start using the microchip tags. Now, if you have no further questions?"

I shook my head and lay down on the pillow, spitting out the pill as I pulled up the bedsheet. Any self-respecting kid knew how to hide a tablet under his tongue, a tablet I was pretty sure had nothing to do with curing headaches. And I did have a further question for Klimt, but I kept it to myself. While he'd been talking, I'd looked for any sign of flecking in his eyes. If there was anyone I suspected of lying, it was him. But I must have been too tired or too scared he'd notice, because I couldn't see a single flicker of movement or detect any signs of emotional feedback.

As if he had no soul.

Or didn't really exist.

Klimt was right about the police. They called again on my first day home, the same two detectives that had talked to me before. This time they gave themselves names: Detective Probert, the man, and Detective Coverley, the woman.

The four of us sat in the living room. Josie, despite her Sherlock tag, was not allowed to listen in and had gone to her room in a huff to phone Tirion.

The police asked how I was and had I remembered anything more about the accident, particularly the car? I shook my head but told them I had something to say. Detective Coverley leveled her gaze. I gripped Mom's hand and told her I was sorry, that I'd lied about being on the headland to see a friend that morning. I didn't mention Candy Streetham but instead told a half-truth. I said I'd gone to the Nolans' house because I wanted to know how Trace was doing, and I'd learned about Rafferty's death from Aileen Nolan. I said it had spooked me a bit. When Mom asked why I'd hadn't said this at the hospital, I lowered my head and muttered, "I thought you'd be mad, because you were so fed up with hearing about the dog."

"Oh, Michael," she sighed. She raised my hand to her mouth and kissed it.

Klimt would have been proud. It was a pretty good act.

The police seemed to accept the lying as standard. But if I thought I was in the clear, I was wrong. The whole session was about to go in a direction I wasn't expecting — literally. Detective Coverley said, "So you were cycling home from the Nolans' house when the car hit you?"

"Yes," I said. Another lie. Suddenly, I felt very cramped and awkward. I couldn't find anywhere to put my hands. I noticed Detective Probert watching me, and that just made the fidgeting worse.

Using a pencil end to check back through her notes, Detective Coverley came out with another observation. "That's not consistent with the accident report. The tire marks we found suggest that the car was coming from Poolhaven toward Holton. Also, the front wheel of your bike took most of the impact. Both these facts would imply you were riding toward the Nolans' house, not away from it. Do you want to comment on that?" She stared at me without a flicker of emotion, a gaze that could strip a coat of paint from a wall.

"Michael?" Mom prompted.

I swallowed hard. Here was a chance to blow the whistle on Klimt and go back to being a normal kid. But I heard myself saying, "My cap came off. I went back for it."

The police exchanged a subtle glance. Detective Probert shrugged, which I understood to mean he'd accepted what I'd said. Detective Coverley tried a different approach. "So you went to the house and spoke to Aileen Nolan?"

I nodded.

"Did you meet Dr. Nolan?"

I shivered, though I wasn't sure why I felt chilled. I gave a quick shake of my head.

"Why are you asking him that?" said Mom.

Detective Coverley crossed her legs at the ankles. She rested her notebook in her lap, stroking the fingers of a ring-free hand. "How did you know it was the Nolans' dog?"

I gulped and looked up at Mom, who was frowning. "Well, tell them," she said.

Detective Coverley threw me a phony smile. The last time I'd seen a grin like that was on the face of the child catcher in *Chitty Chitty Bang Bang*.

"Someone at school told me."

"Freya Zielinski?"

I chewed my lip.

"I'll take that as a yes," she said. "How well do you know Freya, Michael?"

"She's in my class. We're . . . friends."

"Good friends?"

I shrugged.

Detective Coverley smiled again. "Are you aware that Miss Zielinski's father made a complaint to us about Dr. Nolan and his conduct toward Freya?"

"I'm sorry, what has this got to do with Michael's accident?" asked Mom.

Detective Probert raised a hand. "This won't take long, Mrs. Malone. Let's hear what Michael has to say, shall we?"

"Michael?" the woman prompted.

"No," I said. And that was the truth. Freya had never mentioned anything about a complaint.

Detective Coverley reached into her bag for a folder. She took out a photograph and put it on the coffee table in front of me. "Have you ever seen Dr. Nolan speaking to Freya?"

I glanced at the photograph. Liam Nolan was a proud-looking man with a rounded face and receding reddish hair. I shook my head. I'd never seen him before.

But Mom had. "Hang on. Isn't he a doctor at the

Poolhaven practice? I didn't realize you meant *that* Dr. Nolan."

"You know him?" Probert asked quietly.

"Not personally," said Mom. "But Thomas — my husband — went to him once or twice."

"What?" I said. Dad had known (or met) Rafferty's father?

Detective Coverley picked up the photograph and held it up for me one last time. "So, just to clarify, you have never met the man in this photograph?"

"No," I said. But *Dad* had. Why did that make me feel uneasy?

"All right. Thank you." She slid the photo back into the file.

A sudden knock at the door just then almost had me leaping out of my skin. Even Mom put a fluttering hand to her chest. "Josie, get that, will you?" she shouted.

Regaining my composure, I said, "You banned her, Mom, remember? She'll be in her room."

It might be days before we saw Josie again. She could yap for hours once she got started.

Detective Coverley stood up and straightened her skirt. Turning to Mom, she said, "We'll be leaving now. Please feel free to answer the door."

The rap came again.

"Yes, right," Mom said, a little hot, a little flustered. She was about to say "thank you" but stopped herself. Maybe she was thinking it wasn't done, to thank the police for grilling your child. She slipped tamely out of the room.

Detective Probert stood up, making the seat cushion wheeze. "We won't need to speak to you again, Michael. Take care on the roads from now on, won't you? Wear a helmet, not a cap." He clapped a hand against my shoulder and turned to go, beckoning Coverley to follow.

The policewoman extended a hand for me to shake. She reminded me in some ways of Candy Streetham. Not so pretty, but twice as devious. And like Candy Streetham, she was hard to shake off. "One last question," she said.

"We're done here," said Probert in a cautioning tone. He looked toward the hall, where Mom could be heard chatting with the postman.

Coverley ignored him. "Think carefully before you answer, Michael. Do you know of any reason why anyone might want to hurt you?"

"Detective Coverley," hissed the man. He was angry with her now.

"N-no," I stuttered, but my mind was pulling down memories from the headland. What was it Klimt had said? *There are people out there, other organizations, who would stop at nothing* . . . I'd thought little of it at the time. I was just a kid on a grand adventure. Now his words sank in like poisoned raindrops huddling together at the bottom of my soul. I felt sick and ran to the kitchen.

"What's happened?" I heard Mom saying.

Detective Probert replied, "Michael's gone to get a drink of water. It's natural to feel unsettled after an interview. He'll be fine. Thank you for your time. We won't be troubling you again. It's highly unlikely we'll find the person responsible for the accident, but if Michael should remember anything else, please don't hesitate to get in touch."

I heard the front door close. Mom came through to the kitchen.

"You all right, love?"

I turned and flopped back against the sink, my mouth full of foul-tasting saliva.

She stepped forward and pushed my hair out of my eyes. "Don't fret. This will go away in time. We have to put it behind us now, like we've dealt with our . . . troubles in the past. You're safe, that's all that matters. Safe and entirely blameless. Whoever did this to you will have to live with their guilt for the rest of —"

"I hate him," I said.

She let out a sigh. "Oh, Michael. You mustn't feel like that. It was a terrible thing the driver did, but —"

"Not the driver," I snapped. A tear wet my cheek. "Dad. I

hate *Dad*. For not being here. For leaving us. If it wasn't for Dad, this wouldn't be happening."

"What?" she said, sounding hurt and confused. "Your father's got nothing to do with this."

"He has!" I screamed, barely inches from her face. "This is all because of him! This is all his fault!" Then I did the weirdest thing ever. I ran to the room he'd used as his office and hammered on the door and cried, "Come out! Wherever you are! Stop hiding!" And I hammered more and more until the strength went out of me and all I could do was scratch at the wood. I wept and implored him one last time, "Dad, come home. Just please come home."

And I sank to my knees and sobbed. And when I found Mom's arms, she was sobbing, too.

We talked, awkwardly, me and Mom. We sat in the room with the echoes of my dad, and she encouraged me to tell her anything I needed to, good or bad, quiet or loud, whisper or scream. "Let go," she said. "Just let go." I said I missed him at times like this, but I would miss her more if she weren't around. That just got her blubbering again. When we finally dried up, we burst out laughing and told each other what a mess we looked. After that, a sweet sort of calm descended. Mom pulled two tissues from her sleeve and we got to work cleaning our faces. "One day," she said, "we should decorate in here. Move a few things out. What do you think?"

I nodded quietly. I knew what Mom was getting at. It was time to let go of Dad for good. I sniffed and looked around. The place had barely changed in the last three years. His old vinyl albums were still stacked against the wall, all the classical music he'd liked so much. Beethoven, mainly. Wagner. Mozart. It had once been a rule that when the music was playing, Dad was working and you didn't come in here. I'd hated it then; I missed it now. My gaze drifted to the big oak desk that Dad himself had built into the alcove, a green leather chair tucked underneath it. Mom had always thought I might use the desk for doing my homework, but I couldn't ever bring myself to sit in Dad's place. She had emptied its deep drawers long ago, but there were still some bits and pieces on the top: the pen holder Josie had bought Dad one Christmas, the desk lamp that looked like a wading bird, a paperweight gathering dust.

"Shall we get rid of that?" I asked. I pointed to a framed print hanging above the desk on the alcove wall. As well as classical music and opera, Dad had liked abstract art, and it didn't come much more abstract than this. It was a kind of psychedelic drawing of a tree set against a plain gold background. The trunk of the tree and the earth around it were decorated like a patchwork quilt. Six main branches divided into smaller ones, all of them ending in neat brown whorls. There were no green leaves, just occasional strips of what looked to me like bunting flags (though Josie had always insisted they were crowns). Every now and then, a thing like an acorn, or possibly a fruit, grew upright out of one of the branches. And in the body of the tree, low down on the right, sat a tall, dark bird. I had never asked Dad what kind of bird it was because whenever I'd looked at the picture in the past,

I'd always assumed it to be a crow, even though its tail feathers were tipped with white.

"Oh, no. I like the print," said Mom. "Maybe I'll move it into the living room."

"Mo-om? Come on. It's hideous."

She pursed her lips and had second thoughts. "Hmm, maybe you're right. It will only remind me of your accident."

"Sorry?"

"You remember Dr. K from the hospital?"

"Yes," I said, warily. How could I forget?

"The day I brought you home I asked him what the *K* stood for. It's the same as the artist who painted that." She pointed at the print.

Curious, I stood up and went to look. In the corner of the print, in small black lettering, was the name . . . "Klimt," I whispered. The air in my lungs seemed to turn to dust. I looked at the title. *The Tree of Life*. By Gustav *Klimt*.

Mom nodded. "Odd coincidence, no?"

I didn't know what to say. Did this *mean* something? Some reference, some clue to Dad's work with UNICORNE? "Why did he choose this picture?" I asked.

Mom shrugged. "Because he liked it, I suppose."

"But —?"

"Anyway, come on," she said, standing up. "Anytime now,

your sister's going to surface. I don't want her to find us mop-
ing about in here, red-eyed and sniffing. Oh, and while I've
got your complete attention, what do you want for your birthday? I think you're old enough now to choose."

I turned to look at her.

"Speak," she said, after the third second of silence. "Ask,
and thou *might* receive. No promises."

"New bike?" I said.

She drew a sharp breath.

"We have to put the accident behind us, remember?"

"Don't push it," she laughed, poking my chest. She licked
a tissue and wiped away a tearstain I'd missed. "*The Tree of
Life*," she sighed, looking wistfully at the print. She put a kiss
on her fingers and blew it into the branches behind me. "Love
you, Thomas, wherever you are." Her eyes misted again.
"You, too," she said, pinching my cheek. "New bike." She
smiled to herself. "We'll see."

I really missed my bike that week. My return from the
UNICORNE clinic had coincided with a half-term break.
Eight days of recuperation before I could go back to school.
By the end of day two, my brain was dissolving with bore-
dom. I had, by then, looked up *The Tree of Life* online,
thinking I might learn something about Dad's connection to

Amadeus Klimt. But there was nothing. Just a lot of stuff about Art Nouveau.

Then there was the added frustration of not being able to go and see Freya, or even talk to her. I didn't have her number and she wasn't in the book. And although Mom said I could have friends over, the names she suggested were all male. There was nothing I could do but sit it out.

To make matters worse, I had to put up with Josie and her latest new friend. One morning, a virtual clone of Josie, but with slightly darker hair, turned up. I had the misfortune of answering the door.

"Hi, I'm Mystique." She had a smile as wide as a slice of melon and teeth the size of mah-jongg tiles. She was carrying a wrapped box under one arm. A jigsaw by the look of it, or maybe a board game.

"Miss what?" I said. Something about a type of wood?

Her eyes sparkled like a couple of snowflakes. "Hey, are you Josie's brother?"

"No, they found me on the step one Christmas."

"Really?"

I smiled. It seemed the polite thing to do. I'd heard that girls who think they're nice-looking sometimes adopt a less attractive friend. Trust Josie to go for a pal with an IQ lower than the number of days in February. I widened the door. "You'd better come in."

Josie appeared, almost wagging a tail. They did a little air-kissing dance. As Mom entered the scene "Miss Teak" asked, "Can I use your bathroom, please? I'm desperate."

"Upstairs, first door on the right," said Mom.

The wooden one grinned and bounded up the stairs.

Mom soft-shouldered the door. "So . . . what happened to Tirion, then?"

"Too many issues," Josie sighed.

Mom raised an eyebrow. My thoughts exactly.

"Do all your friends have weird names?" I asked. "Don't you know any Marys or Suzys or Pollys?"

Josie gave me her special look, the one reserved for inferior brothers and people who hate her favorite pop stars. "You are so retro," she said, and swished up the stairs like Cinderella.

It got worse. With nothing better to do, I headed into the living room to pick up my book. I was trying to work my way through *The Catcher in the Rye* because I didn't want to get too far behind in English. I'd added a couple more pages to my tally when Josie came in, leaned over the sofa, and whipped the book right out of my hands.

"Hey?!"

"I need you."

"I'm busy. Give that back."

"Misty's brought her Monopoly set. It's no good with two. So you've got to play."

"I don't want to play Monopoly. I want to read, thank you."

"Right, well, I'm gonna tell Mystique to tell everyone at school that you only change your underwear twice a week."

"I so do not!"

"So do," Mom muttered, breezing past.

Thanks, *Mother*. "Look, I don't care if Miss whatever-she's-called thinks I roll in doggy doo. I am not playing Monopoly. GIVE ME BACK MY BOOK."

Josie slapped it onto the coffee table, out of my reach. "Okay, be a grumpy guts all your life." She waltzed by and stuck out her tongue. "By the way, Mystique lives next door to Freya."

"Really?"

"Yep."

"No kidding?"

"Nope."

"I want to be the banker."

"Done."

Cool.

It was a lie, of course — well, a dark shade of white. I had to let Mystique own half of the properties before Josie would bring up the subject of Freya.

"Hey, Misty, you know that goth girl who lives on your street?"

On your street? I mouthed.

Just go with it, Josie mouthed back.

"Freya? Yeah. She's SO weird." Said the girl in the bright pink sweater with white epaulettes. A starry wand and a pair of false wings were all she needed to complete the look. She bobbed a judgmental head. "But in a good way. I kind of like her."

"So does Michael. He's going out with her."

The fairy child dropped her shoulders.

Oh, no. This couldn't be true. That wasn't surprise I was seeing on her face; it was disappointment. She had a crush on me. Help! "B&O Railroad. Two hundred dollars," I muttered.

Mystique bit her lip and reached for her considerable wad of money. She counted off the notes in small denominations, applying poison to each with her thumb.

"He's not allowed to see her out of school," Josie said. "The excitement would probably crack a rib."

"Sixty, eighty . . ." Mystique counted.

Josie rolled the dice. She landed on CHANCE and took a card. "He wants to know if you'll take a message to her?"

What? I eyeballed Josie again. She grinned like an alley cat. She was loving this.

"Oh, look, prison again," she sighed, sliding her top hat there. "Honestly, I am *so* bad."

Misty looped her hair and handed me my money. She picked up the dice cup and plonked it by my knee, creating an earthquake on Mediterranean Avenue. "Your turn."

I rolled the dice and moved my flatiron nine places clockwise.

Josie sucked in through her teeth.

Wouldn't you know it? I'd landed on Boardwalk.

"That'll be twenty thousand dollars," said Misty.

"You win," I said, shoving every bill I had her way. "You're good at Monopoly, aren't you?"

From the corner of my eye, I saw Josie raise a thumb. Compliments. Way to go.

Misty looked down, braiding the ends of her hair. "We could play another game, if you like?"

"Tomorrow," said Josie, "after you've taken Michael's note. You can bring Freya's answer back then, can't you?"

Misty plaited on for what seemed like hours.

"Course, it won't do him any good," said Josie. "He never has much luck with girls." She whirled her hands. *Rope. More rope.*

I couldn't believe I was about to say this. "Yeah," I sighed. "Josie's right. I don't think Freya's really . . . the one, but . . . you have to try, don't you?"

Mystique looked up and nodded in agreement.

Honestly, it was a wonder lightning didn't strike my flatiron.

I kept the note short.

> *I'm sorry about what happened. I didn't know Candy would send me the article. I can explain about Rafferty. Please reply. Michael.*

Three days, another three games of Monopoly, but no word came from Freya. Misty, to be fair, had done her part. Unsure of exactly where Freya lived, she had hovered along their road and finally put the note in Freya's hand, saying that if Freya wanted to reply, she'd be at the bus stop every morning at ten.

She didn't see Freya again.

School opened.

Ten minutes before first period, I saw Freya at the lockers, putting away her coat. She didn't see me until she closed the locker door.

"Jeez, Michael!" She put a hand on her heart. Rafferty's heart.

"Sorry, I . . . didn't mean to scare you."

"Well, you did. And you seem to make a habit of it. Bye."

"Freya, wait." I grabbed her arm.

She shook me off angrily.

"Did you get my note?"

"It doesn't matter about the note." She wrapped her arms around her textbooks and backed away. "Look, I'm sorry about your accident and everything, but I've moved on with my life, okay?"

"But I want to make up with you. I want us to be friends."

By now, other kids were aware of our spat. Suddenly, one of them waded in. "Hey, get off her, Malone."

I thumped back against the lockers, pushed there by none other than Ryan Garvey.

"What do you want, Garvey?" I launched myself back at him, pushing him as far as the opposite wall. "This is a private conversation. Get lost."

"Stop it!" cried Freya, trying to come between us.

But he came for me again, wrestling an arm around my neck, trying to bend me down so he could knee my face. Kids whooped and hollered and offered their advice. "Knee him, Ryan!" "Kick him, Malone!" Around and around the corridor we danced. A useless knot of arms and legs. I'd seen fights like this a dozen times and they usually came to nothing or were stopped by a teacher. This time, my time, I stomped on Ryan's foot and he let me go. He squirmed right around and met me face on — and walked into a perfect rabbit punch. *Smack!* Right on the bridge of his nose. It was the first time I'd seriously hit anyone. The other kids gasped. Ryan didn't cry out. He just slid down against a radiator, blood running through his hands.

"What have you done?" wailed Freya. She crouched down and slipped her arm around his shoulders.

I stood there, not knowing what to do. I felt bad about hitting Ryan, and weirdly confused about what I was seeing. Freya's next sentence clarified everything.

"Go away. I'm going out with Ryan now, all right?"

"Teacher!" someone shouted.

The crowd scattered like a flock of pigeons. I looked

down the corridor. Mr. Besson was approaching. A woman I didn't recognize was close behind him.

"What is going on here?" Mr. Besson thundered.

I couldn't believe it. Ten minutes back to school, and I was looking at another lengthy suspension.

Of all people, Freya came to my rescue. "Ryan's having a nosebleed, sir." She made Ryan stand.

Mr. Besson clucked. "Oh, is that all?" He took out a handkerchief and handed it to Freya. "Nose pinched, head between legs. If it hasn't stopped running before the first lesson, make sure he gets to the nurse. And I'd like my handkerchief back when you're done."

"Sir," said Freya. She dragged Ryan away.

Mr. Besson turned to his colleague. "I'm so sorry, Ms. Perdot, not the best way to start a school day."

"Nothing I have not seen before," she said.

It was the z she put in *nothing* that gave her away. Her blond wig and glasses had thrown me at first, but the soft French accent was unmistakeable.

Chantelle. How had UNICORNE managed that?

"Ah, Michael," Mr. Besson said. "I suppose I should be glad to see you back. We were all very shocked to hear about your accident."

"Yes, sir," I gulped. I couldn't take my eyes off the "new

teacher." She was wearing a stylish black suit and peach-colored top, with a skirt that flared like a mermaid's tail.

"This is Ms. Perdot, who's with us as a substitute teacher. Mrs. Francombe unfortunately broke her ankle during term break. We're lucky to have Ms. Perdot on such short notice. Well, off you go, boy. You don't want to take root."

And we parted company, Chantelle and I.

I was five yards down the corridor when I heard someone wolf whistle. Oh, boy. French with "Ms. Perdot." That was a lesson I could not wait for.

I caught up with Chantelle at morning break. She was alone in Mr. Besson's classroom, smiling at the contents of a French textbook. "The things they teach you to say here, Michael. Next time you visit Paris, be sure to stop the first person you see and tell them, 'My pan of vegetables is boiling over.' I'm sure they will find it illuminating."

"I need to talk."

A boy's face appeared at a window. "That's her," I heard him chatter to his buddies. Already, the new French teacher was causing a stir. Chantelle walked over and closed a blind. "In here," she said. "Quickly. Before someone sees." She gestured to a small supply room. I followed her in, squeezing past a stack of reference books and Mr. Besson's cycling gear. She put the light on and closed the door. "Be swift. Besson might return at any moment. What do you want to say?"

I preferred you brunette? Maybe not. "There's a problem with Freya. She's dumped me for a guy called Ryan Garvey."

"Ah, young love," she sighed, gathering her false hair into a ponytail. "Always so very complicated."

"It's not funny, Chantelle."

"Ms. Perdot," she reminded me.

"I mean it. You saw how scared she was at the clinic. She's avoiding me now. She won't talk about Rafferty while she's with Ryan. And there's no way I'll get her to the Nolans' house."

"Then the answer is simple; you must win her back."

"How?" I threw out my arms and nearly knocked a tray of paper off a shelf.

Before I could say another word, Chantelle had pressed a finger hard against my lips. "Ssssh. I thought I heard something."

Besson, talking to a kid. "Emily, do you know where Ms. Perdot has gone?"

"No, sir," said the girl.

Chantelle leaned forward and whispered, "Garvey is the boy who was bleeding, yes?"

I nodded.

"Okay. I will deal with it." She squeezed past me, switching off the light as she opened the door.

"Ah, there you are," said Besson. "I was worried we'd lost you."

"Oh . . . *non*," I heard her say, acting surprised. She closed the door, shutting me in the dark. "Forgive me, Monsieur Besson, I was simply exploring."

"Shall I take you through the layout of the supply room?"

My heart missed a beat. If he found me in here, we were both finished.

"Later, perhaps. I would like to see the library, if I may?"

"Of course. Of course. Please, after you."

Their voices faded into the distance.

I gave it twenty seconds, then opened the door a crack. There was a girl in the room. She had her back to me, bent over a notebook, writing. I crept out and closed the supply room door, only to knock Mr. Besson's chair. The girl turned. She was the young and studious type. I snatched up a book. "Came in for this. Didn't want to disturb you. Homework assignment."

She glanced at the cover. "That's a first-aid manual."

So it was. Drat. *Think, Malone, think.* "Yeah, I need to know . . . how to stop a nosebleed."

The girl gave me a look that said she *could* have told me, but why would she want to bother? "Make sure you bring it back or I'll tell Mr. Besson you stole it." She tossed her hair over her shoulder and returned to her writing.

Teacher's pet. Nice.

I made my way quickly out of the room, leaving the first-aid manual on a shelf. I wouldn't be needing that — unless I had to rough up Garvey some more.

I had to wait until the final period of the day before I learned how Chantelle planned to "deal" with Ryan. I was back in Mr. Besson's room, with the whole class, including Freya. Chantelle was teaching our French lesson while Mr. Besson looked on from the side of the room.

After hearing our names and saying something to each of us in French, she said, "In a moment, I would like each of you to take ten minutes to write down as many French words or expressions you can think of that are commonly used in the English language. You might be surprised how many there are. *Café*, for instance — you are not allowed to use that for your list."

"Oh!" cried a couple of disappointed voices.

Mr. Besson chuckled. "Come on. There are plenty more. I've thought of half a dozen while Ms. Perdot was speaking."

Of course you have, sir. Anything to impress the gorgeous new teacher.

"I know one," hissed a voice to my left.

Annoyingly, despite our dustup, I was still the closest student to Garvey's desk.

He cupped a hand around his mouth. "*Je t'aime*," he whispered. "It means 'I love you.'"

Clearly, losing some blood from his nose had not affected his "stupid" gene. It was a French phrase, yes, but not what you'd call "in common use." "Yeah, well, I don't love you," I hissed back.

He scowled and aimed a kick my way.

"Garvey! Malone!"

Oh, great. Now he'd done it. Besson had ears like *un grand lapin*. He stared at us over his folded arms. "Pay attention to Ms. Perdot or you'll both be staying after school tonight."

"I was only telling Malone that I knew one," griped Ryan.

"Well, let's hear it," said Besson. "This ought to be good."

Yeah, *really* good. Ryan's face had turned the color of a ripe tomato. Either he was about to confess his undying admiration for Mr. Besson or I would have to rescue the pair of us. Maybe I owed him, for that punch.

"*Au pair*, sir," I said. "Ryan thought of *au pair*."

Someone slammed down a pen. "Aww, *I* had that!"

I looked across at Freya. She sighed and shook her head.

Chantelle made her way down the room and perched on the corner of Ryan's desk. "Very good," she said to him, her voice like a warm summer breeze.

"Thanks, ma'am," he mumbled, barely flicking me a glance before fixing his gaze on Chantelle's huge eyes.

"I will look forward to seeing what else you come up with."

Lauren Shenton covered her mouth and snickered. "Ms. Perdot, Ryan's *useless* at French."

"Apparently not," said Chantelle. "And you are ... Lauren, is that right?"

Lauren nodded and chewed her lip, fearful now that she'd spoken out of turn. She was the class mouse, small and pretty with feathery blond hair. The rumor on the playground was that Lauren liked Ryan, despite the fact that she'd openly dissed him. Chantelle, I thought, had picked up on that.

She looked at Ryan again with a smile that could have melted chocolate. "Well," she said. "*Lauren*, it seems, has thrown down a challenge. Do you think you can do better than *Lauren* with your list?"

A little bubble of air popped out of the center of Garvey's lips.

The class burst into embarrassed laughter, except Freya, I noticed, and Mr. Besson.

"Oh, dear," sighed Besson. "You seem to have mesmerized him, Ms. Perdot."

And maybe she had. It looked to me like Chantelle was glamouring Ryan. His gaze was pinned to her like a moth to a board. But what was she trying to make him do? And why had she put so much emphasis on Lauren's name?

It wasn't long before we found out.

Mr. Besson snapped his fingers and told us to get on with the exercise.

I didn't find it easy. After five minutes, I'd only gotten two: *cliché* and *prairie* (only because Mom had told me once it was French for *area*). But Ryan was scribbling away like he'd worked out the plot of a novel. There was no way he knew that many French words.

And he didn't.

After ten minutes, Besson clapped his hands and told us to stop writing.

Chantelle then asked who would like to read their list.

A small forest of hands went up.

After the teacher's pets had had their turn, Chantelle turned to Ryan. She invited him to stand up and read his list. Ryan shook his head.

"Come on," said Besson, "we're all agog."

Ryan shook his head again. He seemed to have emerged from a mild coma and broken out in a deep, deep panic. He folded his paper and tried to hide it in his bag.

Mr. Besson wasn't having that. He strolled across the

room and snatched the list out of Ryan's grasp. He read it in a flash. "Oh, for goodness' sake!" he thundered, and ripped it into shreds.

But not before Amy Cooper had risen from her seat and peeked over his shoulder. Her horrified gasp kind of said it all, but the details sped around the class like a sizzling, unstoppable gunpowder fuse. *He's written Lauren's name, over and over!*

BOOM! Poor Ryan. He never stood a chance.

The bell rang for the end of the lesson.

First kid out the door was Freya, looking like she wanted to murder Lauren Shenton.

Chantelle caught my eye as I made my way to the front. "*À vous*, Michael," she whispered.

For once, I didn't need a translation. Chantelle had played her part.

Now it was down to me to make up with Freya.

I thought about it all night long. How do you regain the friendship of a girl who doesn't trust you anymore — especially when you have no real recall of just how close you might have been? Even with Garvey out of the equation, there was little chance Freya would talk to me, let alone accept a mumbled apology. I needed a gesture. Something that would move her. Not flowers or chocolate. That would be lame. A teddy bear always made Josie soften, but given the mood Freya was in right now, she'd probably hang a teddy from the nearest tree. I couldn't put a cuddly toy through that. *What do you give an angry goth?* It's not the kind of question Google can help you with.

The answer came to me during breakfast. I'd all but settled on the safe but dull idea of a card, when I had another strange memory flash, the first since leaving the UNICORNE clinic. I saw myself holding a crown of dragons. It was such a distinctive image that I dropped my spoon into my cereal bowl, splashing droplets of milk over Josie's arm.

"Oh, thanks!" She spooned half a Wheato back at me.

A crown of dragons. Where had *that* come from? I picked the Wheato off my shirt and slowly ate it.

"Michael? *E-yuck*." Josie pushed the rest of her breakfast aside.

"Will you help me with something? It has to be quick."

"I'm not washing your shirt, if that's what you think."

"No, not the shirt. How do you make a paper chain?"

"What?"

"A paper chain. You know, like . . . Dad's dragons."

Josie eyed me suspiciously. "Is this for Freya?"

I urged her to keep her voice low. Mom had gone to put some stuff in the trash can, but the breakfast table wasn't out of range. "Yes."

She mulled it over for a moment. "When do you want it?"

Cue best cheesy grin. "Um, this *morning*?"

She sighed and pushed herself away from the table. "How long?"

I glanced at the clock. "You've got ten minutes."

"I meant how many dragons in the chain, doofus?"

The trash can closed with a clatter. "I don't know. Enough to say . . . 'I miss you.'"

Josie did a double take. "Look at you being all romantic."

Mom stepped into the kitchen. "Josie, if you've finished, go and brush your hair."

"You owe me," Josie whispered, and shot upstairs.

She made an amazing chain, out of some Christmas wrapping paper, the good kind that doesn't go limp or tear. The snowflake design on it somehow added a touch of class. I counted twelve dragons when the chain opened out.

Before leaving the house, I found an envelope and a small roll of tape. My idea was to put the dragons in the envelope, seal it, and stick it to Freya's locker door, with no indication that the chain had come from me. But what if she thought Ryan Garvey had sent them? I couldn't take that chance. So when I got to school, I slipped into an empty room, turned the dragons plain side up, and wrote my cell number on them. That used up ten in the chain. I put my initials on the last two dragons, along with a hopeful x.

Then I sealed the envelope and waited.

She was there, in three of my four lessons, but she didn't ever look at me and she said precisely zilch.

I checked the lockers at break. The envelope had gone. Even so, I started to doubt she'd seen it. What if someone had stolen it, thinking there might be money inside? Or what if Freya herself had simply flushed it down a toilet?

Girls: such a nightmare.

I consulted Chantelle. "Give her time," she advised.

I gave her till three fifteen p.m. I looked for her after school. No sign.

In the car, Josie gave me a silent dressing-down. *How could you possibly mess up?* she mouthed.

I buried my face in my hands.

Josie was right. I really didn't have much luck with girls.

The call came at ten p.m. I was in bed by then, unable to sleep. I dived across the room and grabbed the phone. It had to be either Freya or Klimt.

It was Freya.

"I can't sleep," she said. She sounded pretty wired. I judged the mood right for once and let her speak. "She won't let me rest. She never lets me rest. She fills my head with stuff I don't know. Her stuff, things she wants me to remember. I don't know who I am anymore. If I look into a mirror, it's her I see. The girl in the paper, hurt and angry. She has blood in her hair. So much blood."

"Her name is Rafferty Nolan," I said.

Freya started to cry.

"Trace is her dog. That's why she comes to you. You've got Rafferty's heart."

There was a clunk as if she'd dropped the phone, or maybe just fallen onto her side. Through her sobbing, she said, "How can you *know* that? How can you know her name? Even my dad doesn't know who my donor was."

I chewed my lip. How much to tell her? Whatever it was, it had to be convincing. The kind of convincing that might stop a girl from stepping over a cliff.

"I had a transplant, too."

Now I understood Klimt's reasoning. A transplant operation was something few people would have experienced. No wonder he'd kept me on Freya's case.

"I don't . . . remember things about my donor," I said, "but Mom says I was different after the treatment."

"What was it? Your transplant?"

"Bone marrow — for leukemia."

"Do you have to go for checkups?"

"Not anymore."

"Pills?"

"No."

She started crying again. I guessed she went for lots of checkups, probably took a lot of medication, too. That would explain the days off from school. And the sickly skin. And the baggy eyes. The looking-after-her-father thing was probably just a story to keep the hounds at bay; the truth was, her dad was looking after her.

"I still don't understand," she said. "How could you know who my donor was?"

I took a deep breath. This was going to be difficult. One word out of place and I'd lose her forever. "I went to see Rafferty's mother. Not about you, just to check on Trace. She told me . . . how Rafferty had died." I heard Freya sniff, but what she was taking for a sympathy pause was really me wanting to skirt the question of how I knew Rafferty had carried a donor card. In the end, I just ignored it and said, "I kind of guessed you'd got Rafferty's heart. When you freaked in the clinic, I knew for sure."

There was another pause, longer than the previous one. "Who else have you told?"

"No one."

"Honest?"

"Cross my h — Honest. I swear."

"What about the mother?"

I shook my head. "I've only met Aileen Nolan once."

"But does she *know*?"

"No. She's just . . . sad, and confused about Trace."

A small volcano erupted in my right ear. Freya blowing her nose. "What did she tell you about how Rafferty died?"

"She fell off her bike and hit her head on a rock. It was an accident. Why?"

"There was a light," said Freya.

"What?" My hand seemed to freeze around the phone.

"Just before she falls, she looks back — and there's a light. I remember it, Michael. She makes me remember. Someone was following her. It wasn't an accident."

At last, I had something to report to Klimt. A light in the darkness before Rafferty fell. Headlights? I asked. What else could it be? Full on? Dipped? How many? What layout? Freya wasn't certain. Rafferty only had a sense of it, she said. A sudden intense blossoming of light, as if beams had collided from different directions. Maybe a pale blue tint.

At school the next day, I found Chantelle in the languages lab and told her. She nodded and said I'd done well. She warned me not to share this information with anyone, but we both knew my mission didn't end there. In a sense, it was just beginning. If someone *had* been following Rafferty, we needed to know who, and we needed to know why, if only because that same person might have been the one who had driven into me.

Chantelle said, "You have my number. I need to know where you are at all times now. Once you push a stick into a hornets' nest, the wasps get frightened — and people get stung."

"Can't you trace me?" I said.

She looked at me over her fake glasses.

"The unicorn," I whispered, pointing at my feet. "Klimt said there was a tracking device under my skin."

She picked up some student notebooks and started arranging them in name order. "That would be for emergencies only."

That didn't sound wholly convincing, as if she were holding something back, but when I tried to query it, she cut me off, saying, "A call or a text tells me where you're going to be. Forewarned is forearmed, *d'accord*? Have you spoken to Freya this morning?"

"No. She wasn't at registration. I haven't asked her yet, but I think she'll go with me to the Nolans' house now."

Chantelle gave a thoughtful nod. "Tell me when you have set something up. What about the journalist woman — have you spoken to her since the accident?"

"No. I've been meaning to ask you about her. Did Klimt check her out?"

"Check her out?" she repeated.

"He said Candy wasn't driving the car that hit me, but apart from you, she was the only person who knew I'd be on Berry Head that morning."

She put aside the handful of books she'd been stacking. "Are you suggesting that *I* ran you down?"

I gulped and shook my head. Briefly, I'd looked for flecks in her eyes. But there wasn't enough time to get an accurate impression.

"Good. I'm glad you trust me, Michael. You might be grateful for my backup one day."

A bell rang, making me jump.

"Run along," she said, waggling her fingers in the direction of the door. "And don't go beating up any more friends. I would not want to have to put you in detention."

"Yes, *Ms. Perdot*," I said cheekily. Was it me, or was she taking this teacher disguise a bit *too* literally?

"Text me. Regularly. At least once a day."

I hitched my bag onto my shoulder, blowing her a kiss when I thought she wasn't looking.

"*Dans tes rêves*," she said coolly. *In your dreams.*

Oops.

Here's an odd thing about kids of my age. No matter how hard you try not to form a clique, it still happens by association. What I hadn't realized until I punched Garvey was that an act of aggression redefines the borders. Boys — and some girls — who had never really wanted to know me before started opening conversations or hanging out around my space. Some on the periphery drifted toward Garvey. One or two left us both well alone.

And now, because we'd fought over Freya, her status had changed from weird girl to cool — unless you were Lauren or one of her pals, who would have had Freya burned at the stake for practicing the dark art of stealing my affections.

Getting time alone with Freya wasn't easy. She didn't turn up at school again till Friday mid-morning, and was immediately surrounded by three hangers-on. But such was her standing with the geek crowd now that when she saw me hovering like a limpet near the science building, she dispatched one of the gang with a personal message: *She wants to see you in the library at afternoon recess. Who's a lucky boy?*

I felt tense, not lucky. Our last conversation had been pretty emotional. For all I knew, she was going to bludgeon me with a volume of Dickens and tell me to get out of her life for good. When I found her, she was sitting at a desk in a corner, pulling Josie's paper chain through her fingers.

"This was sweet," she said as I sat down opposite her.

I shrugged and said, "I knew you like dragons."

She laid them on the table, smoothing them out with her slender fingers. "Actually, I didn't, until the operation." She dipped into her pocket and pulled out a small, spiral-bound notebook. I'd seen it before. Everyone had. She was often bent over it, sketching like crazy. It was one of the icons that defined her as weird.

She put it down in front of me. "Open it," she said.

I turned it around with the point of a finger.

"It won't bite you, Michael."

But it looked as if it could. I opened the first page. A pencil sketch of a dragon in flight. Its wings were all wrong in proportion to its body, but there was something strangely compelling about it. It looked like the work of a disturbed child.

"They get better," she said, turning the pages herself. She found a close-up drawing in purple ink. Just the head and jaws, in astonishing detail.

"Wow, that's amazing. Have you always been good at art?"

She sat back, chewing a fingernail. "They're hers."

"Rafferty made you do this?"

"Um," she said. "I couldn't draw a stick man before I got this." She pointed to her heart. "She likes dragons and all kinds of mystical stuff. Purple is her favorite color."

I remembered the dragon on the bookshelves at her home. Purple, like this one. It could have *been* this one. "Wow," I said again. This was freaking me out.

"She's been trying to make me draw people, too."

"Old ladies?"

"What? E-yuck. Don't be weird."

"I'm not. Her mom told me she liked drawing old ladies."

"Well, she's changed." She closed the notebook, leaving her hand on the cover. After a moment, she slumped back into her seat and said, "It's all my fault."

"Why? What do you mean?"

"It was me who brought us here."

"To Holton?"

She nodded. "I drove Dad crazy until he caved in. A few months after the operation, I started having this recurring dream. I was standing on a cliff with my arms wide open, catching the last rays of the evening sun. It came so often that I started telling Dad that I wanted us to live by the sea. My dad is the sweetest man ever. He lost my mom when I was six years old and since then, he's given me anything I want. At first he didn't think moving would be possible, because of his work and stuff. But the more he said no, the more demanding I got. I said there had to be seagulls and open green spaces. A place where people like to walk their dogs. And so he brought me here, right into her territory. That's when the drawing — and the visions — began."

"You really see her — in the mirror?"

"I think so. When I'm stressed. It's hard to describe. She's sort of there, but not there, like the blink of a lighthouse. She doesn't like it if I try to force her out. It's cool about the dragons; I always wanted to draw. But when she starts trying to show me what happened that night . . ."

I swallowed hard. "Do you know who was following her?"

She shivered and shook her head. "We're in the dark and it's cold and we're moving fast. She's not particularly scared, but she keeps looking back. There's nothing in the darkness, not for ages. Then a light appears as if someone's thrown a switch. Then I feel her falling and falling and falling, until there's nowhere left to fall and it all stops."

I gulped and looked at the chain of dragons. What would Dad have done in this situation? Maybe nothing more than I was doing now. I couldn't imagine what life must be like for Freya, but if we were going to solve this file, we had to go *deep* into Rafferty's territory. "Will you come to Rafferty's house with me?"

She folded her arms. "That's a bit weird. I'm not sure I could cope. And my dad wouldn't like it. He and Mr. Nolan don't exactly get along. Anyway, what good would it do?"

"She's haunting you, Freya. She's not going to rest until we find out what she wants."

"Oh, and that's really going to work. Knock-knock. 'Hello,

Mrs. Nolan. I'm Freya, the girl who drives your dog nuts. Do you mind if I come in and exorcise the ghost of your scary daughter?'"

"It wouldn't be like that."

"How then, Brains?"

"I promised her mother I'd talk to you about Trace. We don't need any better reason than that."

"Trace," Freya said. She put her head back and looked at the ceiling.

"She knows you, doesn't she? She senses Rafferty in you?"

I watched a ripple run down Freya's neck. "The stupid thing is, I used to be allergic to pet hair. So I trained myself young not to care about dogs or cats or bunnies. Then Trace turned up and it was like . . . where have you been all my life? If I did go to the house, it would be mainly to see her."

"What if he's there?"

"Mr. Nolan?" She shrugged.

"What's he like? Did you feel a connection to him?" I nodded at the region of her heart.

She glanced away. "He's very . . . what's that word? Brusque. I was spooked when Trace kept running to me, but Dad's reaction was a bit over-the-top. He can be overprotective sometimes. He doesn't like me getting stressed, for obvious reasons. And no, the only connection I felt was to Trace. Why do you think that is?"

A bell interrupted us before I could reply.

"Better go," said Freya. She gathered up the notebook and the paper dragons. As she pushed back her chair, I still hadn't moved. "What?" she said, seeing me watching.

"Nothing. Well, I've been meaning to ask. Are we still . . . ?"

"Still what?"

She gave me THE GOTHIC STARE, a 6.1 on the rictus scale.

"It's just . . . I'm not sure, if we're . . . y'know . . . ?"

"We were," she said, "then you got dumped for scaring me witless."

Dumped. Right. Get over it, Michael. "So is Garvey . . . ?"

"Majorly dumped."

Right.

She waltzed around to my side of the table. Leaning close to my ear, she whispered, "Have you ever wondered why girls like guys a bit older than themselves?"

Now she'd morphed into Josie. Wonderful.

Then came the surprise.

"All right. I'll go to the Nolans' with you. The thought of it scares me half to death, but I'd like to be walking around with a heart less haunted. I'm not staying if it feels too weird. Dad won't be home till eight. So I can go after school. You'd better look after me, Michael."

"I will. I promise. I'll need to phone Aileen."

I felt her hand on my jacket collar, folding it down into its proper place. "I really liked the paper dragons; thank you." She kissed her palm and tapped me lightly on the head. "So did Rafferty. That's from her, not me."

The one thing I hadn't thought through was Mom. The prospect of going to the Nolans' was exciting, but asking for permission to cross the headland again was bound to generate a lot of sparks. I knew I'd need backup, right from the start.

So I asked Freya home for tea.

I got the impression when Mom first saw her that it was one of those "defining moments" of her life (a phrase I'd heard her use sometimes). It began with a conversation through the car window. "Hi, Mom. This is Freya. Can she come for tea?"

"Awesome," said Josie, who was already making space in the back of the car.

Freya attempted a smile. She didn't have a coat and was hugging her shoulders against the cold, looking like a little lost scarecrow in the rain, her hair sticking out like a chimney sweep's brush.

"They're going out, Mom," Josie explained.

"Oh," said Mom. A really big life-defining *oh*.

"And they're getting soaked," Josie added.

Mom found her voice. "Yes, well, I'm not really sure if . . ."

"Thanks, Mom," I said, and climbed in beside her.

Freya shivered on the pavement for a moment, giving Mom the chance for a last-gasp getaway.

Get in, I mouthed.

Freya looked doubtful. "We're just friends," she said to Mom, and got in next to Josie.

"Hi," said Josie.

"Hi," Freya replied, somehow managing to shorten the word.

"*Love* the hole in your tights."

I heard a shuffle and guessed Josie was checking Freya's legs. "Thanks. Took me ages to get that right."

"Neat," laughed Josie. The pair of them high-fived.

Even Mom managed the tiniest grin. She hit the turn signal, waiting for a chance to move out of the line of cars. Her eyes went to the rearview mirror, checking Freya, not looking for traffic.

Freya took the hint. "Just so you know, I'm gluten intolerant."

Mom immediately stalled the engine.

I sighed. This could be a long journey home.

Josie snickered into her hand. "She's not always like this. It's because you're the first, so it's a bit of a shock."

"We're just friends," Freya and I repeated. I could feel my face going bright red.

"Don't worry. I get it," Josie assured Freya. "Mom'll get used to you. Won't you, Mom?"

"Gluten —" Mom said.

"Free," said Freya.

Mom patted her hands on the steering wheel. "Right."

As soon as we got in, I made an announcement: "Me and Freya are going up to my room."

"We are?" muttered Freya, in synchrony with Mom, who said, "I'm not sure that's appropriate, Michael."

"We're only looking up stuff on the computer."

"Yeah, right," said Josie, flopping down cross-legged on the sofa. She turned the TV on.

Mom stood defiant. "You can use my laptop — down here, please."

I sighed heavily. This was ridiculous. I was a UNICORNE agent! I bet Amadeus Klimt didn't have to do as he was told by his bossy mother. "Where's the phone book?"

"By the phone," she said, "where it's always been." She pointed to the only landline we had.

It was going to be one of those nights. A battle for supremacy, which Mom was currently winning.

"Thank you," said Freya, coming over all polite. "It's for me, actually, Mrs. Malone. I need to find a telephone number."

Mom's attitude changed in an instant, as if she'd been sprinkled with gothic fairy dust. "Oh, right. Well, help yourself, Freya. Um, would a baked potato be all right for you, for tea?"

"My favorite," she said. "Especially with cheese."

"I think I can manage that," said Mom. She drifted into the kitchen.

As soon as she was gone, Freya whacked me lightly and mouthed, *Be nice.* She was right. If we were going to make it to the Nolans' tonight, we were going to need Mom very much on our side. She had the car keys, after all.

Freya asked the question halfway through tea. We'd done all the usual background stuff about where did Freya live and what were her best subjects at school and what hobbies did she have and what were her future aspirations (Aspirations? Hello?), when suddenly she said, "Mrs. Malone, can I ask you a favor?"

"You can call me Darcy, if you like," Mom said. She was warming to her — but it was early days yet.

"You know the dog that made Michael famous?"

"I do," said Mom, clearing away a plate.

"I play with it sometimes on the headland."

The piece of baked potato on the end of my fork suspended itself in Michaelspace, resisting the gravitational pull of my mouth. Where was Freya going with this? The plan had been for me to do the tricky stuff.

"Do you?" said Josie, driving her hands between her knees. "It's a brilliant dog."

"Siberian husky. The best," Freya said.

"You know the family, then?" Mom inquired, falling deeper into Freya's trap.

"Oh, yes," said Freya, perking right up. "I've met Mr. Nolan lots of times, but I've never met his wife. I've got an invite, though." Casually, she opened a small pill bottle, shook out two tablets, and swallowed them with a drink of water. "Ear infection," she said. "Such a pain."

We all gave her a moment of silence. Me, especially. I was pretty sure the pills weren't for her ears.

"So . . . what's the favor you want to ask?" said Mom.

Freya hit her with a smile Chantelle would have savored. "I know it's a bit cheeky, but would you drive us up there tonight, me and Michael?"

Mom did that parental laugh, the one where they kind of cough a feather off their chest. She coaxed up a weak excuse. "Freya, you can't just turn up on someone's doorstep and . . ."

"We've already called her," Freya jumped in.

I buried the potato and hoped not to gag. She was taking a real chance now. Before tea, we'd looked up Aileen's astrology website and gotten a contact number. I'd phoned Aileen in secret from the bathroom. She'd said yes to tonight, but only if Mom agreed, and could we wait till about seven o'clock, when Liam would be home from work?

Liam Nolan. The thought of meeting him made me shiver.

Everything now depended on Mom. She dug in her heels and came out with a classic. "Michael has homework to do, Freya."

Tough call, but Freya was swiftly on top of it. She dipped into her bag and pulled out a textbook. "We both do. I said I'd help him with his quadratics. Then we can go, if it's okay with you? Just for half an hour."

Brilliant. Pure GENIUS. Mom was on the mat. "And Mrs. Nolan is definitely all right with this?"

I got the stare.

"She's cool," I said, picking up my drink. I sucked a mouthful of juice through my straw so I wouldn't have to say another word.

Mom went into herself for a moment. "And you've met Dr. Nolan, you say?"

"Doctor?" said Freya.

I looked at her. "Apparently."

"Only . . . ?" I knew where Mom's mind was headed, that police interview where all we'd seemed to talk about was Liam. But again, Freya had planned an answer.

"Oh, you heard about Dad's tomato plants, then?"

"Tomatoes?" Mom said.

Freya faked a laugh. "Trace got into our garden one day and made a REAL mess. Dad was SO annoyed. You can't imagine. He went ON and ON about people who can't control their dogs. He's calmed down now, of course." She flapped a hand. "So will you take us?"

Mom was lost for words. I looked at Josie, who was totally in awe of the whirlwind that was Freya.

"Half an hour?" said Mom.

"On the dot," Freya promised.

"Are you happy about this, Michael?"

"I'll look after him," said Freya.

"Um," said Mom, meaning, *That's what I'm afraid of.* "All right. But I take you and I pick you up. No messing about on the headland. Is that understood?"

"Aah, no time to hold hands," Josie giggled.

Mom did not respond well to this. "You. Kitchen. Washing up. Now."

"*What?*" squeaked Josie. "I never wash up."

"Then it's time you started."

And that was that. We were set to go.

I looked at Freya and she at me. *Phew*, she mouthed.

Exactly.

We did go to my room to do our math homework. Somehow, that made it all legit. It didn't stop Mom coming to check on us twice — first with the offer of a cup of tea, then those essential bits of clean laundry that had to be put away before morning. Alone, Freya and I talked tactics. She was still having doubts about what a visit to the Nolans' would achieve.

"What if it makes Rafferty more agitated?"

"Why? We're trying to help her."

"By invading her space and putting her this close to a mother she can never touch or talk to again?" She made distancing movements between us with her hands.

We were sitting on the floor with our backs against my bed, all quadratic equations solved. "We need to find out who was following her," I said.

Freya drew up her knees. "Her parents aren't going to know, are they?"

"We might get a clue."

"How?"

"I don't know." I lobbed a pencil across the room. "But if we don't go, we'll never know, that's all I'm saying."

She sighed and dropped her forehead against her knees.

"It was someone with a black car, and maybe blue headlights."

I felt her twitch. "How do you figure that?"

"Ryan told me ages ago that some cars have these fancy xenon lights that shine a kind of —"

"No, I mean, why should it be a *black* car?"

Then it struck me. She didn't know yet that there might be a link between the two accidents. The look on my face told the whole story.

"Oh my God. You think that whoever went for Rafferty might have come after you as well?"

"It's possible," I said.

She twisted away from me and started rocking gently on her knees. "This is really scaring me, Michael. What if we're walking into some sort of trap?"

I screwed up my face. "Aileen Nolan wouldn't hurt you. She loved Rafferty."

"What about him, though? *Doctor* Nolan."

Our eyes met. She had a point.

"I've watched a lot of detective programs," she said. "The first people the police suspect are the parents."

"Then they've talked to the parents already, haven't they?" I shuffled over and knelt in front of her, until our knees were just about touching. "All we're gonna do is show the Nolans you're okay with Trace — and see what happens."

"And what if Rafferty shows up?"

"She's not going to throw stuff in her own house."

"I mean in *me*, Michael?" She pointed to her face. "She changes me. She makes the birthmark come."

I got brave then and picked up her hands. She was right. I didn't know what was going to happen. I had no answer, other than touch. "I'll look after you, Freya. We're in this together."

"Well, that's very obvious," said a voice from the door.

I dropped Freya's hands like a pair of hot stones.

"In what together?" said Mom.

Yet again, Freya came to our rescue. "Homework club," she said meekly. "I'm helping him with math, he's helping me with history. If I don't get my grades, I might have to drop to a lower class. I get a bit weepy about it. Michael's being really supportive, aren't you?"

"Um," I grunted. Boy, this girl could work a parent.

"I see," said Mom. "Well, it's a quarter to seven. If you want this lift, you'd better get moving."

"Bathroom," said Freya, skipping out of the room.

I stood up, face-to-face with Mom.

"What?" I said, trying to duck the invisible searchlights of her mind.

"I'm proud of you."

"You are?"

"Don't waste the chance of a compliment," she said. "You can be very thoughtful when you want to be. I'm pleased you're helping Freya with her homework. It's a very kind thing to do. Just promise me you won't let any . . . other thoughts distract you."

Like a secret organization, a tattoo on my ankle, an unpredictable ghost, or a potential hit-and-run killer?

Nah.

"We worked really hard tonight," I said.

"I know. And that's just one of the reasons I love you."

Oh, no. Not the kissy thing again. Yep, right on top of the head.

"I'll wait for you downstairs."

Which left me time for one last thing.

I took out my phone and quickly texted Chantelle.

Going 2 Nolans with F

She texted right back: *Time?*

Now, getting a lift

I waited, but there was nothing else.

Not even a smiley French face.

The rain was almost slashing through the Rover's windshield as we pulled up beside the Berry Head cottages. Freya peered out anxiously, running her gaze over the Nolans' house. She'd been noticeably quiet throughout the journey, but I could hardly blame her for that. Not only had we driven past the very spot where Rafferty had fallen from her bike and died, Freya was now about to meet the dead girl's parents.

"Eight?" Mom said. "Or are you going to call?"

Some leeway. Cool. "I'll call," I said. I turned to Freya. "Ready?"

She nodded and opened the door.

Mom waited with the engine running, but there was never any doubt that Aileen would be there. I could hear Trace howling before we'd reached the gate. A piece of stained glass above the door lit up. A fishing boat on a stormy sea. Freya shuddered and felt for my hand.

"You don't have to do this," I whispered.

But we did. Aileen had already opened the door and was

beckoning like crazy for us to get out of the rain. We ran ten yards and were in the house. The door closed with a tinkle of wind chimes.

Rafferty Nolan's heart had come home.

"What horrible weather," Aileen said. She smiled at Freya, but there was no recognition either way. Freya threw a startled glance toward the kitchen. On the other side of the kitchen door, Trace was scratching like a dog buried alive in its kennel. Before I could speak, Aileen burst forward and hugged me so hard I almost stopped breathing. "Oh, it's so good to see you," she gushed. "You can't imagine how shocked I was when I heard what had happened." She pulled back, bridging her hands beneath her chin. "And you must be Freya?"

Freya had shrunk into a corner of the hall, holding herself so taut and thin that she could have hopped out of an umbrella stand.

Aileen extended a hand.

Freya looked at it as if it were an alien projectile. She had buried her hands in the sleeves of her sweater, adopting what Mom called the straitjacket pose. She looked as brittle as a black rose dipped in liquid nitrogen, ready to crumble at the slightest touch. I was just beginning to think this was all a big mistake, when Freya muttered, "I like your ring." Aileen was wearing what looked like a wedding ring — gold with a small bouquet of diamonds.

"Thank you," she said, withdrawing from the handshake.

"Why is it on your right hand?"

Personal, but Aileen did respond. "It's from my first marriage."

I glanced at her left hand. There was a plain gold band on her third finger. So who was Rafferty's father, I wondered, the first husband or the second?

"Liam's been delayed at work, I'm afraid, but he should be home any minute. He doesn't know you're coming. Please be tolerant if he seems a little gruff. That's just his way. I'm sure he'll be fine. Why don't you both go into the living room before Trace digs a tunnel out of the kitchen?"

I stepped forward and guided Freya by the elbow. She had turned milk white and was beginning to breathe in nervous snatches. This was not a great start. Aileen must have been wondering what she was doing, letting this awkward girl cross her threshold. I wondered if she'd checked her charts for vampires that day.

I stepped into the living room and drew Freya in. She immediately took another sharp breath and laid both hands across her heart.

"Is she here?" I whispered.

Freya shook her head. "The music."

From a small stacking system on the sideboard opposite came a few eerie notes of piano music, played as lightly as puffs of smoke. It was a classical piece I'd heard before on TV commercials. In the middle section, the notes rocked back and forth like the perfect accompaniment for a monster creeping up from behind: *de-dun, de-dun, de-dun, de-dun, de-dun-dun*. I liked it, but I couldn't tell if Freya did or not. She had drifted toward the upright piano and was dragging one finger along the keyboard as if the music were coming out of there by magic.

"Here we are," said Aileen.

Trace swept in like a furious patch of tumbleweed. She ran straight into Freya, knocking her into a sitting position on the larger sofa. She thumped her paws onto Freya's knees and frantically set about licking the visitor. Far from being scared or overwhelmed, Freya wrapped her arms around the husky, soaking up her frantic need for comfort. If dogs were capable of crying tears, Trace would have produced a tsunami.

"My goodness," said Aileen, clutching a star-shaped pendant at her neck, "that *is* a powerful bond. Um, sit down, Michael. I'll go and put the kettle on while those two . . ." She ran out of words.

I perched on the edge of an armchair seat. "Aileen?"

"Yes?"

"What's the music?"

"Satie," she said, unable to take her eyes away from Freya. "Gnossienne number one. It was Rafferty's favorite performance piece."

With that, she slowly backed out of the room.

"I've missed her so much," Freya said quietly.

"What? Sorry?" I twisted toward her.

She clutched the ruff of fur around Trace's neck and looked right into her pale blue eyes. "I love you. I'll never leave you again."

What? Was this Freya talking or Rafferty coming through her?

I glanced at the bookshelf in the conservatory. Nothing appeared to have toppled over and the temperature in the living room hadn't dropped ten degrees. No sign of Rafferty's presence — yet.

"How do you want to play this?" I whispered. "What do you want to say to Aileen?"

"I need her, Michael. She has to be with me."

"What? What are you talking about?"

"Trace," she said. "She has to be with me."

"Freya —?"

"You told me they were thinking of getting rid of her."

"Yeah, but —"

"So why shouldn't I have her?"

"Because . . ." But I couldn't think of a reason to oppose it. It might even be the solution the Nolans were looking for. But just in case Freya didn't understand that the random abduction of dogs was illegal, I said, "Okay, we can ask — but let me do the talking."

"Whatever," she said, as though the outcome were already decided. She had grown in confidence since Trace came in and was about to step it up a significant notch. "Here," she said, "take her a moment."

She tried to pass the dog over, but Trace stayed glued to her side as she stood.

"Freya, what are you doing?"

She pulled out the piano stool.

I looked toward the kitchen. Aileen wouldn't be long.

"Freya, you should ask before —"

"Shut up," she said. "I need to hear."

She placed her fingers over the keys, touching them as if she were cracking a code, but not yet making any sound. Then, just as Aileen appeared with a tea tray, Freya played three notes, not in time with the stereo, but in perfect tune.

Aileen froze on the spot. Now she was the one losing color from her cheeks.

I opened my mouth to say something but was stopped by

the ring of my phone. I dug it out of my pocket. The letters *AK* lit up on the screen. Klimt.

"Sorry, I . . . I need to take this." I stood up, hovering over Freya. She was staring rigidly at the keyboard. Her hands were now at rest, in her lap.

Aileen blinked and came back to herself. She put the tray down on a coffee table. "Yes, of course. Go and sit on the stairs. The reception's better on that side of the house. It will give me a chance to . . . get to know Freya."

"I won't be long," I said to Freya.

She didn't move.

This was getting seriously weird, but I couldn't ignore the call any longer. So I scurried out and sat on the bottom of the stairs, taking the call as I steadied myself. "I'm at the Nolans'," I said as quietly as I could. "Freya's here with me. What do you want?"

"Has Rafferty appeared?"

"Raff —? *No.* I can't talk about this now. They could hear me, Klimt."

"I want you to meet her again," he said.

Again? "What are you talking about?"

"The next level, Michael."

The small hairs on the back of my neck stood up like a row of iron filings.

"There are strong similarities between the movements of

spirits and your ability to jump across the temporal interface. This is a unique opportunity to study the boundaries between our world and theirs. I'm going to attempt to send you to Rafferty. If things become difficult, focus on the UNICORNE symbol. That will bring you back."

"Look, I don't have *time* for this. I'm kinda busy right —"

Before I could finish, a high-pitched tone came down the line, sending tendrils of sound into the core of my brain. The line went dead. I felt a sudden jolt, as if the world had stopped spinning. When it started again, Rafferty Nolan was standing in front of me.

28 · PEELING

"Michael!" she said, clapping her hands in glee. "Wow!"

I gaped at her in silence. She was dressed in a pair of khaki-colored cargo pants with straps hanging off the combat pockets. On top was a hoodie, too short at the waist, sitting over a plain white T-shirt. Ankle boots with soft fur linings, laces loose, bunching socks. White hoop earrings, way too big. Hair tied back in a frizzing ponytail. She looked cool, like she was going to a gig. She'd made no attempt to hide her birthmark. I could see no blood on the other side of her head.

"Hello? Rafferty to Planet Michael? You gonna sit there all night or what?"

She shot out a hand.

I reached for it and had the sensation of peeling, as if I'd stripped away the topmost layer of my skin. She gripped my hand and drew me forward, pulling a ghost of me off the stairs. I had left my physical body behind, sitting there rigidly, holding the phone.

"It's all right," she said as I started to panic. "Once you get used to it, it's kinda neat."

"Am I dead?"

She walked over to my body. "Feel this?" She ran a fingernail down "his" neck.

I felt a tingling sensation below my left ear. "Yes."

She clicked her tongue. "Just visiting, then. So . . . why are you here?"

I closed my eyes and concentrated hard. To heck with Klimt and his temporal interface. "I need to know what's going on with you and Freya."

"Holy moly!" she cried. "Look at *that*!"

At the top of the stairs, a pure white unicorn had suddenly appeared, tossing its mane in slow motion. It turned away in a cloud of dust motes and disappeared out of sight. In an instant, Rafferty was standing where the horse had been, looking along the landing for it. "Come on," she called down, "before we lose it. Just think yourself up here. It's easy. Come on."

I shook my head. This was just too weird. "No, I need to go back. I need to make sure that Freya's okay." I could still hear Satie on the stereo, though it sounded like two notes trapped in time, bouncing around in bubble wrap.

Rafferty reappeared right in front of my nose. "You can be with *Freya* in a minute," she tutted, speaking her name like a puff of smoke. "Come on, Michael. You imagineered a unicorn. I LOVE unicorns, especially the white ones. It's a sign over here. They lead you to places. They show you the light. Oh, please help me find it. You did promise you'd help me. If you follow it, you'll get an answer to your question. That's the way things work in this world."

Still, I hesitated. "Just tell me what happened that night. Who was following you when you fell off your bike?"

She stood up straight and folded her arms. "Now you're being boring."

"I don't care. You're hurting Freya. She's scared of you, Rafferty. Tell me what happened and I'll do what I can to put it right. I want to help you. Both of you."

"Then come on," she said, her green eyes sparkling. "Whatever path you create here, you have to follow. We have to see where the unicorn leads us." She grabbed my hand. With a whoosh that felt like a million points of air had passed through my chest, we flashed to the top of the stairs. "Things move fast on this side," she said. "But there's loads of time where you are. Look." On the lower steps, my body hadn't altered; the phone was still pressed against my ear.

"Hey! It's gone to my room. Come on."

"Your room?" I held her back. Even on this side of con-sciousness, there were some things her mother would not have approved of.

"It's just a room," she sighed, rolling her eyes. She clicked her fingers and we were instantly there.

It was no bigger than mine in size, but nothing like as neat as I'd been expecting. There were clothes on the floor, shoes everywhere, headphones and an iPod nesting on a chair, a hair-clogged brush on the bedside table. A room in motion, Mom would have called it. A lived-in room, suspended in time. From a dressing table drawer hung an angel pendant. Rafferty walked across and stroked it with her finger, making it twirl back and forth. "You can touch but you mustn't change things," she said. "That would only make Mom cry."

"Rafferty, tell me —"

I cut myself off. She had just flashed onto the bed, sitting cross-legged with her back to the wall. Above her head were two posters of Paris, one a silhouette of the Eiffel Tower, the other a woman in a brown fur coat at a café table in 1937. Next to them was what looked like a movie poster. Emblazoned right across it was the word . . .

"Amadeus," I breathed.

"Totally love his music," she said.

"Whose music?"

"Mozart, of course." She gave a flick of her shoulders. "Wolfgang Amadeus Mozart. Great movie. Cool poster, isn't it?"

All it showed above the movie title was the silhouetted

head and arms of a figure wearing a cloak and a crescent-shaped hat. It looked to me a bit like a highwayman. Or maybe the phantom of the opera.

"Do you like Mozart?", she asked.

"My dad did," I muttered. The albums at home. Somewhere on them, I was going to find the name Amadeus. First Klimt, now Amadeus. There had to be a connection.

But what?

"Hel-lo?" Rafferty flipped her fingers, making a dolphin mobile spin. "What's the matter? You look like you've seen a ghost — oh, sorry, you have."

Hilarious. Now I knew where Freya had gotten her wit. "Tell me about that night."

"I'm not ready," she tutted, picking at her fingers. "I don't want to leave here yet."

"Leave? I don't understand."

"Yes, you do," she said, resettling her shoulders. "You're a visitor here. That means you can return any time you like. But when this is done, I have to leave." She rested her hand on a pair of white jeans and a college sweater, the only two items of neatly folded clothing in the entire room. "Mom's done the laundry again," she said. "Every week without fail. So sweet. And look, she's bought me a brand-new sketch-book." She moved her hand over a spiral-bound notebook so like Freya's I thought it was the same one. "He took it," she said. A dark tone filled her voice. On the landing, I thought I saw a lightbulb flicker.

"Who?" I pressed. "Who took your book?" I remembered Candy mentioning this in the message she wrote on the newspaper article, Rafferty's notebook disappearing. "Someone followed you home after your piano lesson, didn't they? A black car. Who was driving it?"

She sighed and thumped her head back against the wall.

"I need to know, Rafferty. They tried to kill me, too. My mom's so wired she won't let me out on my own any —"

"He wasn't trying to kill me. He just wanted the pictures."

"Pictures — in your notebook?"

She nodded.

"Who was he?"

"I don't know his name. He wasn't nasty, just pushy. He followed me out of the Holton police station and offered to take me home. I said no."

"What were you doing in the police station?"

She looked out the window at the lightning-filled sky. "Telling them — what I'd seen on the headland. They didn't believe me; maybe he did."

"What did you see?"

She closed her mouth tightly, biting her lip. "Look in

Freya's book. I showed her, Michael. I made her remember. I made her draw it. Freya knows."

"But the only things she draws in her book are — Hang on, you saw a *dragon*? On *Berry Head*?"

I didn't know whether to fall over laughing or order my sword and shield right then, but she wasn't going to help me out either way. She sat up smartly, as if she'd heard a doorbell that only spirits could detect. "Liam's here. It's time. You need to go back."

"Time for what? And why'd you call him Liam?"

"Because he's my stepdad, not my dad."

I heard the sound of tires pressing through the rain as a car maneuvered on the road outside. The engine died, almost taking me with it. For half a second, the car's lights had flooded the window.

They had colored the glass a weak shade of blue.

"Go back," said Rafferty, more urgently now.

My head was spinning. "Why, what's going to happen?"

"I hate that man, for what he did to me. For taking me away from Mom, from all this. If I tell you everything, they won't believe you either. It has to be this way. I've worked it all out. I have to bring everything into the open. Show, not tell. Isn't that what they teach us?"

"Rafferty, stop babbling. Just tell me what you know. Did Liam have something to do with the accident? And what exactly did you make Freya draw?"

"I promise I won't hurt her — not much, anyway. Thank you, Michael, for bringing her to me. I know you like her. But it has to be like this."

She closed her eyes and pressed her hands to the center of her chest.

"No!" I shouted as I realized what she was doing. I immediately pictured the UNICORNE symbol. With a rush, I slammed back into my body. The jolt was so strong I dropped my phone. It skidded down the polished floor of the hall and was batted aside as the house door opened. A tall, lightly bearded man stepped in, carrying a doctor's bag.

"Who on earth are you?" he said. "And what the devil are you doing on my stairs?"

There was a scream from the living room. Somehow, Liam surged in ahead of me and was already kneeling down, tending to Freya, when I skidded up to Aileen's side. "What happened?"

"She fell off the piano stool, clutching her chest."

Freya was on her back on the floor, breathing as if she'd swallowed a baby's rattle.

"Get the dog out of here," Liam said, pulling a stethoscope out of his bag. He fixed it to his ears and opened Freya's blouse. "Has she taken anything or —?" He stopped speaking when he saw her operation scar.

I grabbed hold of Trace. "She has tablets for her heart, but I don't know what they are."

"Her heart?" said Aileen. She looked as though she was going to faint.

"She needs to go to a hospital, now," Liam muttered. He stuffed the stethoscope into his bag and slid his hands under Freya's back. "Aileen, get on the phone to Holton General and tell them to prepare for a cardiac arrest. There's no time for an ambulance. I'm driving her in."

Aileen put both hands across her mouth. "It's her, isn't it?"

Liam rose up with Freya in his arms. "For God's sake, woman, get a grip. Turn this mawkish music off and call the hospital. Now."

"You're not going anywhere with her," I threatened, holding Trace like an attack dog.

Liam looked at me as if I'd lost my mind. "What is wrong with you two? This girl is going to die if she isn't treated quickly. Now put the dog in the kitchen and bring my bag to the car. I'm going to need you to sit with her while I drive. Hurry, boy. Move."

His car was white, an Audi perhaps. Nothing like the one that had hit me on the road. The moment his lights punched holes in the rain, I asked him if they were xenon beams. No, he replied, irritated at being made to think about it. He told me they were a longer-lasting type of bulb that could be mistaken for xenon lamps because they burned with a slight blue flare. They were well within legal limits. Any more ridiculous questions? I was desperate to ask if he remembered Dad, but this wasn't the time. I shook my head. Then let's get this child to the hospital, he said. And though I couldn't say for certain that he hadn't been involved in Rafferty's death, from that moment on, he became Dr. Nolan in my mind, not Liam.

He drove fast, like an ambulance would, spraying water out of puddles and running red lights. He had a canister of oxygen in the car. There was a mask attached, which I held to Freya's nose and mouth all the way. "Just breathe," I kept whispering. "Breathe. Just breathe." I put my arm around her, hoping it wouldn't be the final time. She felt no heavier than a bundle of rags. I would have gladly given her my own heart then. Anything to save her fading life.

The car swept onto the forecourt of Holton General Hospital, where a medical team was waiting with a gurney. They wouldn't let me stay with Freya but said I could sit in the lobby if I wanted to. Dr. Nolan offered to drive me home, but I refused to leave the hospital until I knew Freya was going to be all right. He patted my shoulder and went to speak with some of the medical staff. Within minutes, a nurse appeared with Freya's cell phone. She crouched beside me and asked if I knew the name of Freya's father. She pointed to a contact labeled DADDY. Daddy. It almost made me cry. I shook my head, and the nurse said not to worry, and had I called my parents to let them know where I was? I thanked her and phoned Mom right away. She was surprisingly calm and told me to stay put until she got there. While I was waiting, Chantelle slid into the chair beside me.

"What do *you* want?" I hissed. The last thing I needed now was UNICORNE messing up my life even further.

"I was watching the house and followed you to the hospital. What happened to Freya?"

"Rafferty tried to stop her heart."

"Why would she do that?"

"I don't know. Some sort of weird revenge plan. It's Klimt's fault for making me take Freya there."

"I will call him."

"Yeah, tell him I'm back — and I'm looking for him."

She stared at me hard.

I pulled down my sock to reveal the tattoo. "This isn't just a tracking device, is it? He planted something in me that makes me shift when he plays a signal on a cell phone."

"Cover yourself," she said, wary of the gaze of a passing orderly. "I know nothing about this."

"Bull!"

"Such manners, Michael. Your mother would be so impressed."

"Mom's gonna be here any minute. If you don't disappear right now, I'll make sure she sees this and knows exactly why it's there." I let my sock snap back. "Take Klimt a message. If Freya dies, I'll hold him responsible."

She stood up slowly, looking about eight feet tall in the jeans she was wearing. "Big words for a small boy, Michael. Do not do anything foolish. Trust me, you need me more than ever now."

She walked away without looking back. Barely a minute later, Mom burst through the hospital doors.

She swept through the lobby with her coat flying open and dropped into the seat Chantelle had vacated. She gripped my hand. "Is there any news?"

I rested my head on her rain-sodden shoulder.

"You did the right thing, coming to the hospital with her," she said. "We'll stay as long as we need to."

For half an hour, we drank tasteless coffee from a vending machine. We stared at the sunshine yellow walls and watched cars sluicing in and out of the parking lot. Shortly, Freya's father arrived. He was an ordinary-looking man, with his daughter's dark hair. We introduced ourselves but said very little. He looked shocked and confused, like a man who'd walked onto a film set by mistake. They drew him away, down an endlessly long corridor. We didn't see him again before we left.

I was already losing track of time when a doctor dressed in scrubs with a face mask loose around his neck came to speak to us. Dr. Nolan was with him. Mom gripped my hand. This didn't look good.

The hospital doctor said, "Freya's stable but in a critical condition. She'll be here for a while and we may have to operate. As you're not directly related, I'm afraid I can't tell you any more than that. I suggest you go home. Call tomorrow. We'll have more news then."

"Thank you," Mom said.

"Will she live?" I asked. I couldn't stop a tear rolling down my cheek.

Dr. Nolan stepped forward and encouraged me to stand. "She's in the best possible hands, Michael. Can I give you both a lift home?"

"Thank you, but my car's outside," Mom said.

He nodded kindly. "Then allow me to escort you both to the parking lot."

Mom had parked in the regular slots, well away from the doctor and ambulance spaces. We parted quickly from Dr. Nolan, which meant there was little need to talk, other than a few words of consolation. I thanked him for rushing Freya to the hospital and said I was sorry if I'd said anything out of turn. He just looked at me and nodded and got into his car.

"Come on, let's get you home," Mom said. We walked swiftly to the Rover and pulled on our seat belts. She was about to start the engine when Dr. Nolan's car pulled up, blocking our path. He got out and knocked on my window. I slid it down.

"This was on my backseat. It must have dropped out of Freya's pocket. Probably best if you take it. Good-bye."

He handed me her notebook, the one she'd shown me in the library.

"Thanks," I said, and put it on my lap.

It stayed there until we were on the coast road. Then I couldn't bear it any longer. I switched on a light and opened the book.

"What is it?" asked Mom.

"Some of Freya's drawings."

She glanced sideways. "Dragons?"

"Mmm. She likes them."

Mom nodded. "Talented girl. I liked her — *like* her," she corrected. She frowned and looked away.

I continued turning pages. More and more dragons, until right at the back . . .

Suddenly, I started to retch.

"Michael?" Mom squealed. She slammed on the brakes, then quickly leaned over me and opened my door.

I vomited onto the road. That was one pothole filled, at least.

Mom jumped out and hurried around to my side, producing yet another tissue from her sleeve. "Oh, Michael, baby." She wiped my mouth.

"I'm all right. Honest." I stayed her hand. "Sorry — for the mess."

"It's just the shock coming out. And you missed the car, anyway. The rain will soon wash it off the road." She ran my hair off my brow. "What am I going to do with you, huh?"

"Nothing. I just want to go home, Mom. Please."

She noticed me closing the book and said, "Your hand's trembling. Did something in the book upset you?"

I shook my head. It was a lie, but there was no way I could show Mom what I'd seen.

It wasn't a brilliant drawing but close enough for recognition.

On the inside back cover was a pencil sketch of a human face.

Not an old lady.

A photographer.

Eddie.

There was one other drawing that wasn't a dragon. An eerie sketch of the sea at night with moonlight patterning the rippled water and what looked like a cargo ship in the distance. In the sky above it, the clouds were parting, as though God himself were about to speak. I studied the picture but didn't really get it. All I could think about was that image of Eddie.

Now, more than ever, I needed Chantelle.

So the following morning, I got myself together and asked Mom if I could go into town and meet Ryan. Another lie, of course, but I needed a good excuse to be free.

Josie had a bagel halfway to her mouth. I could almost see her thoughts dropping through the hole. *Ryan? A week ago you were punching his lights out.*

Mom was hesitant. "I thought you might want a quiet day at home after —"

"We're buying a present for Freya."

"Oh. I see."

"I texted the whole crew. I really need to do this."

"Well, that's understandable. All right, I'll drive you in."

"No!"

"Michael?" She looked taken aback.

"I'll be in town, Mom. No one's going to run me down on Hope Street, are they?"

Harsh, Josie mouthed. She bit into her bagel.

I sat down and picked up a cereal packet. "Sorry. I'm just . . ."

"I know," Mom said, tousling my hair. She took a moment to deliberate. "All right, you can go. But call me when you get there so I know you're safe."

I shuffled some Wheatos into a bowl. "Is there any news from the hospital?"

Mom shook her head. She picked up a couple of empty glasses and started heading toward the kitchen. "I called first thing. There was nothing then. They asked me to call again at ten."

I looked at the clock. 9:35. "Mom?"

"Hmm?"

"Which hospital was I in — after my accident?"

Josie pulled another face, but this was important.

"Holton initially. Then you were transferred to a private clinic."

"A private clinic?"

She turned her wedding ring. "You have your father to thank for that. He put a lot of things in place before . . . Let's just say he made sure we'd always be well looked after. Not just with the house, but health care and everything."

"Where was it?"

"The clinic? On the outskirts of Holton. Where the old coal mine used to be. Why?"

"Just wondered."

An old coal mine.

The perfect place to hide a secret organization.

I set off just after ten. There was still no news about Freya. I walked down the drive in my old denim jacket, aware that Mom's gaze was burning into my back. At the end of the drive, I turned left along our road, which was the signal to Mom that I would walk into Holton or catch the bus.

But I wasn't intending to do either.

My plan was to call Chantelle and get her to run me back to the clinic, where UNICORNE headquarters must surely be. I went armed with copies of the drawing of Eddie and the strange sea scene, aiming to show them to Klimt. But it never came to that. The moment I was out of sight of the house, I bumped into Candy Streetham.

"Michael," she said, perking up like a meerkat. "I was just on my way to see you." She was dressed more casually than the last time I'd seen her, in a pair of black jeans and a simple gray jacket.

"Can't stop. I'm . . . going into Holton."

"Fine. Hop in. I'll give you a lift." She gestured to a small red Fiat parked in a spot just along the road.

"I'm okay, thanks." I walked on past her.

"Sorry to hear about Freya."

The words thudded into my back like arrows. I slowed to a halt. "How did you know?"

She overtook me and zapped open the locks on the car. "We get feeds from all the local hospitals. 'Doctor in mercy dash to save transplant patient.' Not the biggest story in Holton right now, but very important to you, I'm guessing." She held a door open. "Come on, I know the best café in town. Thirty minutes, tops. All the cola you can drink. There's cake in it, too — if you're feeling talkative."

She took me to Reynolds, an old-fashioned place with round oak tables and hand-stitched tablecloths. We sat in a sloping, claustrophobic window looking at passersby on Hope Street through glass as misshapen as a jam jar bottom. I had a tall banana milk shake and a slice of carrot cake. Candy had coffee, decaffeinated, black. The only thing she ate was the minuscule biscuit they put in her saucer, and she only took one bite of that.

"So how've you been?" She stirred her coffee with her fingers splayed. "You're looking well. Did you get my card?"

Straw in mouth, I nodded.

"Did it tell you what you needed to know about Rafferty?"

"Some."

She extracted her spoon and dropped it in her saucer. "Why do I get the impression there's more to this than you want to share?"

I took a drink of my shake. It was one of those with ice cream floating in the bottom, the kind you have to suck until your cheeks implode. "Why didn't you come to our meeting on the headland?"

"I did," she said, looking out the window. "I arrived a few minutes after the carnage. By then, it was all flashing lights and twisted metal. It looked nasty. I'm glad you're okay. I mean it."

I knew she did. I was watching her eyes. She didn't care about me much, but she wasn't lying.

"Why were you late?"

"I was held up in traffic."

"On the coast road?"

"No, here. In town. They're still doing work on the water mains. I was running behind with an editorial and misjudged the time — journalistic curse. Eddie suggested I cut along Hope Street because it would be quicker if the lights were kind. They weren't. End of story."

"Eddie the photographer?" My carrot cake suddenly felt heavier than lead.

"Okay, it was a cheap trick faking the photo, but —"

"You told Eddie you were meeting me?"

She shrugged. "He's a colleague. We share information all the time. What of it?" She picked up her coffee, tutting as the table leg rocked a little.

"What kind of car does he drive?"

"A BMW — no, a Ford, I think. He changed it a couple of weeks ago. Why?"

"What color is it?"

The cup didn't make it as far as her mouth. She lowered it back toward the table, seating the bottom in the indent of the saucer as precisely as a satellite docking on its mothership. "What are you getting at, Michael? I've known Eddie Swinton for over three years, ever since he joined the *Holton Post*. He's a friend and a talented photographer. He's not the kind of man who goes running down kids."

"Only you and Eddie knew I'd be on the headland that morning." (As long as I discounted Chantelle and Klimt.) "What if he deliberately sent you through town so he could go via the coast road and reach me first?"

She sat back in her chair, looking like her cheekbones were ready to crack. "Jeez. What the heck's in that milk shake? Have you any idea what you're implying? How serious an accusation that is? You're talking about attempted murder. What reason could Eddie have to mangle your bike?"

"Rafferty."

"What?" That took her by surprise. Her eye colors danced.

"I was starting to ask too many questions about her."

She shook her head. "This is not funny."

"Neither is spending a week in the hospital."

"You seriously think," she lowered her voice, "that Eddie killed Rafferty?"

Not deliberately, perhaps. But I was certain now he was driving the car that had followed her that night.

A phone buzzed somewhere in Candy's bag. She dug it out, rejected the call, and banged the phone down on the table, making it wobble again. "No one's denying you had a nasty experience, Michael, but chances are, you were hit by someone changing a CD or reaching across the seat for their phone. Take your eye off the road for a second and you can have an accident — just like that." She snapped her fingers. "I came here to talk about the dog, not Rafferty. But while we're on the law enforcement theme, I'm going to ask *you* a question. Where was the knock on my door?"

I stuck a fork in my carrot cake and left it speared. "I don't understand?"

"If you suspect Eddie, you must suspect me. Why didn't you tell the police about our meeting? For the past two weeks, I've been waiting for a knock that never came."

"You didn't do it," I said. "You didn't run me down."

"How do you know?" She threw out her hands.

"Because you drive a small red Fiat." And she had the flecks of truth in her eyes.

She sat back, shaking her head in bemusement.

"Did you stop?" I took another drink of my shake.

"What?"

"Did you stop at the scene?"

"Of course I *stopped*." She looped her hair crossly. "I watched them stretcher you into the ambulance."

"What did you tell them?"

"Who?"

"The police. If you've been waiting for the police to call, you couldn't have told them you were there to meet me. So what *did* you tell them?"

"Nothing," she said, playing with her watch strap. "I said I was traveling to Poolhaven on a job and I'd stopped at the scene because . . . it was a story. If you must know, I was too afraid to mention our meeting in case they started asking awkward questions."

"Too afraid? Like Eddie might have been if he knew he'd caused Rafferty to fall off her bike?"

"This is ridiculous." She took a fast gulp of coffee and slammed the cup down. "I should never have brought you here. You're just a kid with a big mouth, Michael. You've got no right to say these things when you haven't got a single grain of proof." She picked a napkin off her lap and threw it down. "Here's a ten." She threw a bill across the table. "If it comes to any more than that, find it yourself."

And she stood up too quickly, forgetting that the table legs didn't quite add up to three. What was left of her coffee somehow found its way onto her lap. "Oh, God!" she cried, bringing the entire café to a hush. "These jeans are Dulcie and Gavanna!"

She snatched up her bag and ran for the ladies' room.

Leaving her cell phone on the table.

Maybe it was because she'd called me a bigmouth. Or maybe I was still too wired about Freya. Or maybe the unicorn on my ankle was telling me here was my chance to close this file. Whatever the reason, I was about to commit the most dangerous act of my entire life.

Ignoring the stares and the whispers from the room, I picked up Candy's phone. It was identical to mine, just one edition newer. I tapped the screen and brought up her contacts, finding Eddie in under three seconds. I tapped the screen again.

New message.

Been talkin 2 the Malone kid. He's saying weird stuff bout Rafferty N. Think u shud hear it. Meet me on the head by the landslide. 1hr

I hit SEND and watched it go. Then I took out the SIM card, dipped it in my milk shake, and put it back.

Across the road was a taxi stand. I knocked on the window of the first available car. The driver folded up a newspaper and dropped his window. "Yes, son."

"I need to go to the cottages on Berry Head West."

I showed him the cash.

"You do a bank job or something?" He looked along Hope Street for a trail of bills.

"Please, I'm in a hurry. You can keep the change."

He stuffed the bill into the pocket of his shirt. "In that case, your wish is my command. Let's ride."

Eddie turned up five minutes before the hour. He didn't bother with the parking lot half a mile away but simply pulled off the road and got out without locking his car. Even from a distance, I could sense his confusion. It didn't look like the willowy Candy Streetham standing in front of the landslide signs. No, it looked like Michael Malone.

He took the embankment in confident strides, looking left and right for unwanted company. Some distance away, an elderly couple was fussing over a couple of dogs. Other than them, and the odd passing car, it was just me and Eddie.

"What's going on?" He jutted his chin. He had his hands stuffed into a sand-colored coat, fully unbuttoned despite the wind. There was a hole in one of his black Chelsea boots. He hadn't shaved that morning.

"New car?" I said. It was a gray off-roader. Different in every respect from the black sedan he'd driven into me.

I caught a twitch at the corner of his eye. His gaze flickered beyond me briefly, as if I might be holding his colleague hostage. "Where's Candy?"

"Not coming. I used her phone to send you a message. I thought it would be better if we talked out here, in case you wanted to pay your respects."

"My what?"

"To Rafferty," I said.

Again, he checked left and right. He took another stride forward. I braced myself. The sea and the rockfalls were only yards behind me. "Are you trying to be funny?" He was so close now I could smell on his breath what he'd eaten for breakfast. There were food stains on his sweatshirt, too. "Whatever you think you know, boy, think again."

I stared right into his pale gray eyes. He was a big man, several inches taller than me, but the slope of the ground was bringing us level. His flecks were dancing, popping like crazy. He was anxious, but he hadn't spoken an untruth yet.

"Well?" he snapped.

"I know it was you. I worked it all out. You told Candy that the husky belonged to Freya, but you knew all along it was Rafferty's dog. You just didn't want her name in the papers again. You got lucky when someone mentioned Freya or the argument Dr. Nolan had had with her dad. But all the locals know Dr. Nolan. And they all know he walks his husky on these cliffs."

He laughed and stubbed the toe of one boot into the ground. For the first time, he took his hands from his pockets. Large hands, covered in wispy brown hairs. In a fight, there was no way I'd overpower him. But I wasn't here to fight. I just wanted him to talk. He said, "Let me tell you an old photographer's joke. It's about a man who pretends to take a picture of his wife on a cliff top. When he asks her to step back so he can focus . . ." He made a falling motion with his fingers. "Do you want me to take your picture, Michael?"

I swallowed hard. "Easier than running me down with your car."

He turned his head to one side and chewed on this a moment. "That wasn't meant to happen."

"Tell that to my family."

"It was her fault," he hissed.

"Her?" I prompted.

"*Her*," he said again. "The Nolan girl. She was there, right by the rock where she died. It spooked me and I swerved. You . . . you got in the way, that's all."

I remembered her voice and the warning in it. She had clearly been worried that he might drive into me, but by appearing when she did, she could have unintentionally made it happen. So there was some truth in what Eddie was saying. But his eyes still told a muddled story.

"I was on my way out here to talk to you," he said.

Less gold, more green. But the flecks were interchanging

too fast for me to make an accurate assessment. "To tell me the truth?"

"What truth?" he spat, inserting a swear word between the others.

"Why did you follow Rafferty that night?"

He clenched a fist and came half a pace forward. "I didn't *kill* her."

"But you were there," I said, trying not to be distracted by the particles of food in his yellowing teeth. "She went to the police to tell them something, and you went after her. Why?"

"I was at the station already," he snapped, his face twisting into a knot of anger. "She came in saying she'd seen something — out there, on the water, breaking the waves. A craft far bigger than a submarine."

The second picture. "Craft?" I said.

"The desk sergeant told her it was just a ship. Go and annoy the coast guard, he said. But I'll give the girl her due; she was a feisty little thing. She sat down on a row of chairs, in among the drunks and other misfits, and drew what she'd seen."

"This?" I showed him the copy from Freya's book.

He backed away, startled. "Where did you get that?"

"Doesn't matter," I said.

But it did to him. He stepped forward and snatched it from my hand. "That's not possible. That can't be real. She only drew one —" And he stopped, suddenly, knowing he was about to incriminate himself.

"You took her notebook, didn't you?" I said. "The one with the original drawing in it."

"You need to shut your mouth," he threatened.

"Why?" I pressed. "Why was the notebook so important?"

He held up the picture and let the wind take it. It was fifty yards away in a matter of seconds. "Evidence," he said through gritted teeth.

"Of what?" Interesting. His eyes weren't lying.

He pushed a hand through his ragged brown hair, pulling so hard at a shoulder-length clump that I thought he was going to tear it out. "I just wanted to talk to her," he said. "Get the whole story. Find out what she'd seen. They like that at the *Post*. Anything weird connected to the sea. It wasn't gonna happen there, in the station. So I got into the car and followed her up the coast. I pulled alongside her with my window down. Showed my ID. Told her I wanted to talk about the drawing. She glanced at me briefly, said she wasn't interested, and pedaled away."

He paused and ran a hand across his mouth. Now it was coming, the truth about Rafferty Nolan's death.

Without prompting, he said, "I was closing in again when we saw the light. A beam. Like a spotlight. At a shallow angle. It panned across the headland from above the water. Blue, then red. Flaring in my headlights. It startled her. The bike wobbled badly, to the far side of the road. She put up a hand. Lost her balance. Fell. Then the light was gone. And she was on the ground." He looked down for a moment. I half expected some words of remorse, some regret for his part in Rafferty's fall. But when he started to speak again, his words were cold and matter-of-fact. "I pulled up, but she wasn't breathing."

"She was," I said. "She died in the hospital."

"I *saw* her," he growled. "She was as good as dead. She wasn't gonna survive. Not with half a boulder buried in her head."

"You could have called an ambulance."

He gave a scornful laugh. "And put myself in the middle of a police investigation? They interviewed everyone who'd seen her at the station. It was obvious they thought a car was involved because the girl had died on the wrong side of the road. I told them I'd driven straight back into Holton. They had nothing on me. They couldn't prove a thing."

"You still haven't said why you took the book."

He threw out a hand, as though inviting me to dance. "Haven't you been listening to anything I've said? There was a light, like nothing I'd seen before. She was right, the girl. There was something out there. Something . . ." His voice drifted off into the wind. A moment ticked by, and then he said, "The book was on the road, spilling out of her bag. I just . . . It was evidence. A kind of proof. You hear about these things. Animals mutilated. People being taken. There've been sightings before along these cliffs."

I looked at him and almost felt a touch of pity. It would be easy to suppose that an alien craft had been cruising the coastline looking to beam up unsuspecting humans, but I could think of something far more believable. "You saw a helicopter," I said.

This he dismissed with a snort of laughter. "I'd have heard a chopper."

"Not if it was windy."

He grimaced and turned his head to one side.

"You ran," I continued, "because you didn't want to face up to what you'd done. The UFO story is just a cover. You left Rafferty to die because you're a coward. And you ran me down because I told Candy the truth about Trace and she was beginning to make a connection. It wouldn't have taken her long to find out that the police talked to you about Rafferty's death, would it?"

"I told you, you need to *shut your mouth*." He leveled a malevolent finger. The flecks in his eyes were red, red, red. "You can't prove a thing. And if you breathe another word of this to anyone, I'll make sure your family gets dragged through the mud." He saw my hurt look and laughed in my face. "That's right," he said. "You know where this is going. There were some interesting theories about your father and the reason he disappeared when he did." He nodded his mean, self-satisfied head. "At the time, there was no evidence to support it. But it's amazing how effective a well-placed rumor can be."

"Shut up! My dad would never have hurt Rafferty."

He backed away, tapping the side of his head. "No, but it's what people *think* that matters. Bye, Michael. Oh, one last thing. If you want to see another birthday, don't ever come near me again."

He spat on the ground and turned to go. And that was it. I should have just let him walk. I had him, recorded, all over my smartphone. But I stupidly said, "I won't need to."

He paused and looked over his shoulder.

And wouldn't you just know it, my phone rang.

Right away, he knew he'd been taped. "Hand it over," he said, snapping his fingers. "Nice and easy. Don't make me hurt you."

I took out the phone. Mom's face lit the screen. Mom, wondering why I hadn't called, wanting to know if I was safe in Holton. I felt sick.

"Give it to me. *Now*," Eddie demanded.

No way. I hadn't come this far to let him win.

I rejected the call and put the phone in my pocket. His face twisted into a look of disbelief. Before he could speak again, I dipped into my jacket and pulled out a chain.

"You can't be serious. You think you can take me with that?"

I let the links drop, making sure they rattled. "Not me," I said. "This is a choke chain."

He caught my subtle glance to the right, and turned in time to feel forty pounds of Siberian husky thudding into his chest.

The setup had been simple. I'd asked the taxi driver to drop me off at the Nolans' house. I was gambling that one of them would be home, and Aileen was. We had talked about Freya, and I had told her all the things that Freya had told me, about wanting to live near the sea and finding the sudden ability to draw, but without ever saying that Rafferty's heart was inside her. That I left for Aileen herself to decide. When it got too emotional, and time was moving on, I asked if I could take Trace out — on my own. Aileen had agreed without a second thought. On the headland, I started talking. "I'm going to take her off the leash now, Rafferty. If you're here, I need you to keep her occupied until I call her. You owe me this." And then I had let Trace loose. Seconds later, she was jumping around an unseen hand and chasing invisible sticks across the green. When she saw the spaniel the couple was walking, she had gone to investigate. Rafferty had kept her there, waiting for my signal.

· · ·

But Eddie was strong — and smart. Instead of trying to batter Trace off, he allowed himself to fall back under her weight, using his coat to wrap her head. For a couple of seconds, he lay on his back with her, writhing and cursing as he fought to keep her jaws away from his throat. Only then did Rafferty appear. She was wearing the white jeans and college sweater I'd seen folded up on her bed at the house, the same clothes she'd been wearing on the night she died. Her wavy blond hair was mangled with blood. In her right hand, she was carrying a rock.

Terrified, Eddie kicked back hard, making crescents in the grass with the heels of his boots. "No!" he cried as Rafferty raised the rock.

What was she doing? This wasn't part of the plan. "Rafferty, don't kill him!" I begged. "Stop! They'll think I did it!"

And she faltered, but not because of my plea. She stared into the distance and gasped three times, each breath building on top of the last. The rock fell out of her hand. "Michael," she whispered, and covered her chest.

"Rafferty?" I said, more terrified now than Eddie was.

And she held out a hand to me — and faded away.

The effect on Trace was immediate. She yowled in confusion and tried to wriggle out of Eddie's grasp. Sensing the fight going out of her, Eddie rolled them down the embankment, punched her in the head and threw her aside. The beating didn't seem to harm Trace any, but she was a different dog all the same. She turned a low circle with her tail between her legs, howling pitifully into the wind. Eddie wiped his mouth and staggered away from her, up the slope and back toward me. As we faced each other, my phone rang again.

"Give it," he growled.

I backed into the wind.

His pace increased. "I said give it!"

"No," I said, stumbling on the scarred and bumpy ground. All my options were gone, except one. I took the phone from my pocket — and hurled it behind me, over the cliff.

He swore an oath to the devil and stormed forward, picking me up in a handful of denim, forcing me beyond the signs, to the edge. The sea roared without choosing sides. I managed a half glance over my shoulder. Amazingly, the phone was still ringing. It had fallen among a spill of loose rocks, not far from the old viewing platform.

For the last time, Eddie checked his surroundings. The couple and their spaniel had drifted away. Trace had limped off toward the road.

He pushed me toward the barriers. "Climb over. Down to the platform."

I shook my head. "I'll never reach the phone from there."

"I'm not asking," he said. And he pulled out a knife. Spots of rain made patterns on the blade as he lifted it toward my quivering throat. He flicked it upward, almost nicking my chin. "Climb."

The barriers were nothing but a few metal panels anchored to some hefty crossbeams of wood, just below the point where the drop began. Any kid with a spark of adventure in his soul could have scrambled over them with ease. I reminded myself that Freya had done it on the morning all this began. I whispered her name as I found a hold on an exposed end of wood. If I hadn't been so pushy about us going to see Aileen, Freya wouldn't be where she was now — and nor would I.

"Get a move on," said Eddie.

I straddled the top panel, chafing my thigh as I dropped down the other side, onto the steps. Eddie followed by the same route, making the panels bend and boom. He bustled me around and pushed me down the steps, yelling, "Get up!" when I slipped on a bed of rain-softened lichen. Every footfall raised my heartbeat by five. I was panting by the time we stepped onto the platform.

"Are you gonna kill me?" I turned to face him.

The wind whipped at the edges of his coat. "No," he said. He looked crazy now, edgy. He rolled the knife in his hand and put it away. "We'll let nature take care of that. Put your hands on the rail. The broken one."

I started to shake.

"Do it," he said.

The topmost of the two rails had rusted at one end, leaving holes in the aged metal. As I grabbed it, it creaked a dangerous warning. One good push and it was going to snap. Far below, the waves gathered like a shoal of fish. Underneath the dark tide, the rocks awaited.

"Let me go," I pleaded. "Even if you make me jump, they'll find the phone."

"I don't think so," he said. "One kick and that rubble goes into the sea. You should have let it go, Malone, all the stuff with the girl and the dog. You should have just accepted the fact that the papers get it wrong sometimes. The irony is, I'll probably be the one who snaps the pictures when Streetham writes up your 'tragic' accident."

At that point, I turned from the rail and rushed him. The impact knocked him back against the cliff face. He swore as his head hit the rocks, but the struggle was short-lived and hardly worth it; he was just too strong for me. With one huge shove, he pushed me toward the center of the platform. The boards creaked and the iron supports underneath them lurched, throwing me onto my knees. Eddie stormed forward and kicked my shoulder with the sole of his boot, tumbling me toward the rusted rails. I put out a hand and grabbed the lower rail. It immediately broke, pulling away from the rock and mortar it was once embedded in. From somewhere, I found the strength to snap it from its opposite joint and rap it hard across Eddie's shins. He screamed in agony but came at me before I could hit him again. He grabbed the rail and pressed it across my chest, pushing me against the one last piece of horizontal metal between me and the drop. For the first time, in terror, I let slip about UNICORNE. "Don't do this," I gasped. He was almost crushing the air out of my lungs. "I know people, an organization. They'll look for me and work it out. They'll hunt you down."

He laughed in my face. "You're a weird kid, Malone. If I didn't want you dead, I'd make you front page news. You and your dog and your scarecrow of a girlfriend."

That tipped me over the edge, but not in the way Eddie Swinton was expecting. I couldn't take any more taunts about Freya, not with her lying in a hospital bed. He pushed and the rail behind me broke. But as the dread of that awful fall washed over me, every nerve in my body lit up and I experienced a powerful reality shift, all wrapped up with thoughts of survival and thoughts of Freya. The next thing I knew, everything had reversed: I was on the platform and *Eddie* was falling through the rails. He screamed as the top support gave way and his body folded into the void. I was sure he was doomed, but he somehow managed to throw out an arm and grab the base of an upright with one hand. He swung like a limp flag waiting for a breeze, his fingers turning white as they clawed to keep hold.

"H-help me," he stuttered.

At that moment, I heard the panels boom and saw Klimt's aide, Mulrooney, coming over the barrier.

"Michael!" a woman's voice shouted from above.

Chantelle was on the cliff top, looking down. "Stand back. Mulrooney will deal with this."

But as Mulrooney made it to the bottom of the steps, the whole platform collapsed, taking Eddie with it. Mulrooney flung an arm around my chest and hauled me to safety, turning me away from the sea and Eddie's screams. "Don't look," he said. "It won't be pretty."

I didn't look, but I did hear a distant thud, a morbid sound that would haunt me forever. For whatever reason, good or bad, I had made a man fall to his death.

"We need to get you out of here," Mulrooney said. "It won't be long before someone reports his car."

"H-how did you find me?" I was shivering with fear.

"Your UNICORNE trace. The signal was good in Holton, weaker here, which delayed us. Next time, tell us what you're planning, Michael."

"My phone." I could hear it ringing again. Poor Mom, what had she done to deserve a son like me?

Mulrooney scanned the rocks. "I see it," he said quietly. "Go to Chantelle. I'll get the phone."

Against his advice, I looked down at the water. I could see no sign of Eddie, just a single wooden plank bobbing on the sea. "It's too dangerous. You'll . . ."

"Not for me," Mulrooney said. And he did something quite extraordinary. He moved along the rubble to the farthest point of safety, then squeezed his eyes shut and put out his hand. I heard a scratching sound. Amazingly, the phone jiggled out of the rocks and almost jumped the short space, into his hand. He wiped some algae off the broken screen and handed it over. "Phone your mother," he said. "Remember, you're supposed to be in town."

Back on firm ground, I exchanged a few words with Chantelle and accepted her offer of a lift home. As I walked toward their car, I spotted Trace lying at the side of the road. During the drama with Eddie, I hadn't had time to think about Rafferty and why Trace had given up the fight. Now it began to swell in my mind. I knelt beside Trace and pushed my hand through her fur, whispering, "What's the matter, girl? What is it, eh?" At the same time, I went through the motions of phoning Mom.

"Michael! At last. I've tried three times to get you."

I put my hand on Trace's head. She made a soft mewling noise. "I was in Cloops," I lied, "down in the basement." I'd heard Mom complain that it was hard to get a signal in there sometimes.

"Well, never mind. You're here now." She took a deep breath. "Look, sweetheart, I've got something to tell you. I'm afraid there's no easy way to say this. I had a phone call from the hospital. Freya died ten minutes ago. I'm so sorry. Wherever you are, come home soon. Do you want me to fetch you?"

"No," I croaked, though of course I meant yes. I wanted Mom more than anything right then. I ended the call and threw the phone down. Trace, the road, the grassland, the sky all began to merge into a watery mosaic. As I lowered my head, a tear fell onto a rock where a bunch of wilting flowers had been laid. The tear glistened for a moment, before soaking into a crack in the stone. "No-ooooo!" I screamed, for all the universe to hear.

Two hands slipped gently around my shoulders.

"It's all right," she whispered. "It's all right. It's all right."

And I fell into the arms of Chantelle, and wept.

They held the funeral service at Freya's local church, St. Matthew in the Field, an old stone building chiseled out of the hills overlooking Coxborough. I wasn't sure I'd be welcome, or even allowed to go, but Mom made some phone calls and cleared it first with Freya's father. I had told Mom nothing about Rafferty or her heart, just that Freya had been pampering Trace when she'd collapsed. We learned from Mr. Zielinski that it wasn't the first time she'd had such problems, which was probably supposed to make me feel better. It didn't. I felt responsible for Freya. For the whole of that week, before we went to church, I was under a shadow as black as the unicorn that symbolized Klimt and all he stood for. I had killed two people in the space of a day. And neither of them truly deserved to die.

In church, they described her as "a promising student" with a "uniquely effervescent personality." Her father stood up and said she was a "rare gem," a "daughter in a million." I could have added several tributes of my own. In the short time I had known her, she had made me aware of how great a female friend could be. The closest I had come to that before her was Josie, who stood between me and Mom throughout the service, crushing my hand and sniveling like a dog left out in the rain. I counted twenty-six people in the church. There was no sign of Chantelle, Mulrooney, or Klimt.

As for me, I didn't cry until the very end, when Freya's aunt stood up and read a short poem that Freya had written about her mother. Most of the words floated into the rafters, but two lines opened me up like a well:

I put another rose on your grave today

I miss you in the silence when I walk away

Mom, who was already doing some hopeless origami with a bunch of wet tissues, whispered, "We'll do that. We'll take a rose from our garden and put it on her grave."

And I cried for myself as much as for Freya, because if Mom knew the truth of the past few weeks, there would be no roses.

There would just be thorns.

We didn't go to the burial itself because by then Josie was a walking marshmallow and I couldn't face it, anyway. But five days later, after lunch on a Sunday afternoon, Mom did as she had promised and went into the garden and cut me a single white rose. She wrapped the stem in foil and put it on the sofa beside me. "I think it's time, don't you?"

Time to say good-bye. Time to get on with living.

I nodded and picked up the flower. The scent from it reminded me of Freya. She might have looked like something out of Gormenghast castle, but she always had a faintly floral smell about her.

I said, "Can I go on my own?"

This, I hoped, was a well-timed request. Two days after Freya's death, I had "celebrated" a subdued birthday. I hadn't had a party, but a bunch of my friends had come around for tea, including, wonder of wonders, Ryan.

On the doorstep, we'd put our fists together and ground our knuckles until it hurt. He'd called me an idiot; I'd called him a jerk. Mom, overhearing this bonding ritual, had sighed with false parental joy and said if only she'd kept the reindeer hats we'd worn last Christmas, we could have clashed antlers as well.

Hilarious.

The major present for my birthday was a brand-new bike, even better than the last one, a sign that Mom had moved on from my "accident." I'd ridden it in the yard and the lanes around the house, but here was my chance for a real test.

Mom gave a quick nod. "All right, don't be too late." She tousled my hair. "Tea at five. Ride carefully. Be good."

Be good. What a joke. I didn't deserve a grain of Mom's trust. As the pedals flew around, I kept telling myself that I ought to be feeling slightly heroic. I had solved a complex UNICORNE file and avenged a young girl's untimely death. But what I felt most was an air of detachment. I now lived in a world where deceit was commonplace and fully expected.

I was the monster Mom feared I was becoming.

I was not a nice boy anymore.

The lying, of course, didn't end with Mom. Chantelle and Mulrooney asked me to take them through everything I'd done to lure Eddie to the cliffs. Mulrooney smiled when I said about dipping Candy's SIM card into my milk shake. "You're a natural," he said, and Chantelle added, "I'll deal with the journalist." I took that to mean that whatever Candy knew would be glamoured out of her. Any conversation she'd had with me would be dumped into her mind's recycling bin. I asked them what would happen about Eddie, and would the police come and quiz me again? Mulrooney said, "No one's going to bother you, Michael." And he was right. The next day, a story appeared in the *Holton Post*, describing how one of their photographers, Eddie Swinton, had tragically died taking photographs from the old viewing platform on Berry Head. One of his cameras had been found in pieces on the rocks, but his body had been swept out to sea. As yet, it had not been recovered.

I found Freya's resting place easily enough. Although the cemetery was large and divided by a maze of crisscrossing paths, most of the graves were old and grassed over. The new ones stood out because of their beautifully tilled earth; they looked like a host of skillfully worked molehills.

She was on a slope in a new patch of ground, close to some brambles and a railway line. It was too soon for a headstone, but her name was displayed on a temporary cross. FREYA ANN ZIELINSKI. I liked the simplicity of that.

There were plenty of flowers on the plot already, many with condolence notes attached. I took the rose from its foil and planted it right in front of the cross. I didn't have a note, but I did have a white unicorn I'd cut from one of Josie's mags. I propped it against the stem of the rose and told Freya it was a gift for Rafferty, to lead her to wherever she needed to be. I stood up and lowered my head. The sun passed behind a bank of clouds, fanning the grave with a ripple of shadows. I took a deep breath and was about to say something in Freya's memory, when a voice from behind me said, "Hello, Michael."

I didn't even look round. "What do *you* want?"

"To pay my respects to your friend. What else?"

"You've got no respect for anyone," I said. "Just get out of here, Klimt. I want to be alone with her."

He ranged up beside me and threw a spray of lilies onto the grave. "I warned you this life wasn't easy, Michael. Sometimes there are casualties. Freya's death is regrettable, but it was not your fault."

"Try telling her father that. Or Aileen Nolan. Or Josie, even. Why don't you go back to your UNICORNE coal mine. Leave Freya in peace. And me, too."

He smiled and steepled his fingers. "We both know that won't be possible. Besides, I have to debrief you before we move on to your next mission."

"I don't *want* another mission."

"Of course you do. We have much to accomplish, you and I." A slow freight train clattered past. He seemed to be enjoying the rattle of the tracks, as if it amused him to work out the ratio of wheels to cars. "I assume I'm correct in thinking that you changed your reality during your skirmish with the photographer?"

Skirmish? That was an understatement. I looked down at Freya's grave, then off to one side. A crow had just landed on a headstone a short distance away. It was quickly joined by another. "It just happened, like it did before. He was going to push me over the cliff and I . . ." I covered my eyes; I couldn't bear to relive it. "All she had to do was scare him off. Then none of this would have happened."

"She? Rafferty was with you?"

"I asked her to help me."

"Interesting," he said.

Interesting? "She died as well, for good this time, when Freya's — when her heart gave up."

"But you connected to her plane at will," he mused. "That's impressive. You're developing quite a skill set, Michael. Even your father couldn't summon the dead."

And on that subject, it was payback time. "Tell me about him. You promised you'd say more when the file was solved."

He smiled and pulled his watch from his vest pocket. "When you take the next mission."

"You promised me, Klimt. I'm tired of your games!" In a moment of madness, I tried to strike him. But he moved as fast as the rippling sunlight and clamped my wrist in a grip no human could have possessed.

As I winced in pain, he said, "Do not ever attack me, Michael. I could crush a human arm, including the bone, and terminate you any time I wish. You have already discovered what a telephone call can do, but there are many ways of switching off the quantum trace we planted in your mind. The result, I assure you, would not be pleasant. And please don't imagine you can change your reality and escape my control. You are mine now. A UNICORNE agent. You will do as I tell you, when I tell you. Under my guidance, your skills will develop. Very soon, we will continue our work to help you control your reality shifts. Trust me, it's what your father would have wanted." With that, he let me go. "Take a few days' rest — to get over your friend. I'll be in touch. Goodbye, Michael."

"Tell me about the painting," I snapped.

He hesitated and slowly turned back. "Painting?"

"*The Tree of Life*. It's on the wall in Dad's room. It was painted by a man called Gustav Klimt."

"An odd coincidence," he mused.

I gritted my teeth, holding my wrist across the center of my chest. It felt like it had gone two minutes in a microwave. "We don't believe in coincidence, remember? The albums, too. Mozart. He liked Mozart. Wolfgang *Amadeus* Mozart."

Klimt smiled and moved a twig across the path with his foot. "Save your imagination for your missions, Michael. I need to —"

"I've been remembering things," I cut in. "The laboratory. The octopus creatures in the tank. I thought they were dreams. Really bad dreams. But now I know they're true."

I held up the Meztamine tablet I'd spat out in the clinic. His face turned seriously dark.

"I know what you are, Klimt. I've worked it out. You always talk about humans as if you're not one of us. Dad was far smarter than he ever let on. But he forgot about the eyes, and how I might try to read them one day. You're an android. A machine. He designed you, didn't he?"

He stared at me for two or three moments, before tilting his head in the way I'd always considered robotic but without ever realizing how accurate I'd been. He strode forward, until there was barely space for a leaf to fall between us. His strange eyes, one purple, one blue, locked onto mine. "If you believe this . . . fascinating theory, Michael, then you must accept we have a common bond. For we are no longer looking for *your* father, but *ours*." He gave a curt nod and quickly backed away.

"Tell me something about him! Anything!" I shouted. "I need to believe he's out there still."

Once again he stopped, this time in the shade of a large oak tree, where another crow had landed on a branch above his head. A fourth, I noticed, was on the strip of grass behind Freya's grave. "Very well, I will give you something, though it will only confuse you further. The first time we met, you asked me what your father's last mission was. He did go to New Mexico — to investigate claims of a curious form of DNA."

"Alien," I said. It made me hollow inside, but maybe Eddie was right. What exactly was that craft on the water?

Klimt grunted in amusement. "Not in the way you are thinking of. The DNA sample had allegedly come from a creature whose roots are embedded deep in the human psyche. There are many strange things in this universe, Michael, and much you have to learn about UNICORNE's part in it. That is why you will accept the next mission. This is the last thing I know about Thomas Malone: The creature your father went in search of — was a dragon."

And with that, he finally walked away.

I sank onto a fallen gravestone, my heart thumping like a dull bass drum. Was this another of his cruel hoaxes? Or had Dad really crossed a continent in search of a beast that had only ever existed, as far as I knew, in storybooks and tales of mythology?

I lowered my head into my tired hands. In the last few weeks, I had talked to ghosts, nearly gotten myself killed, reinvented my own reality, and been sucked into a sinister organization that could snuff me out at any moment. When I weighed it up like that, I had every reason to believe what Klimt was saying. But it would take one final leap of weirdness to really convince me anything was possible.

Anything.

Another crow landed on the path beside me. Then another came out of the trees and waddled to the edge of Freya's grave, joining two more that were already there.

Moments later, the shadow of another bird came over and landed directly on the mound of earth. I watched it pick up the unicorn cutout and throw it aside. "Hey!" I cried, and got up to shoo them off.

That's when a voice said, "I wouldn't do that if I were you."

I whipped around.

Sitting on a bench just along the path, holding my rose to her breast, was Freya. She was dressed entirely in black, in a kind of one-piece wrap that shone like the feathers of the birds around her. And though her face was as pale as death, her once brown eyes were as dark as coals. Her hair was wilder than ever, strands fizzing out at the strangest angles, as if she'd had a really bad hair-spray day. Sitting on either side of her were two more crows. "Don't mind these guys," she said, a croak like the crunch of glass in her voice. "You're going to see a lot of my favorite birds now."

I counted ten. And I was only half looking. "You can't be here. You're dead," I gasped.

"I think the correct term is *undead*," she said. "Love the rose, by the way. Very gothic. So who's the geek with the accent? Didn't really like his attitude much. Interesting conversation you were having. We've got a lot to talk about, haven't we?"

"No," I said, "this can't be happening." Yet another bird

swooped down onto the path. I turned full circle. There were crows everywhere. "What do they want?"

"They want me," said Freya, the words almost freezing on her breath. "They follow me, Michael. Don't be frightened. You have nothing to fear. You're my maker. I can't ever hurt you and nor will they."

I shook my head. "Maker? I don't understand."

"Oh, I think you do," she said. A cold light entered her opaque eyes. "Welcome to your dark inheritance, Malone."

And she morphed into a crow and took off with the rest of them, into a blaze of golden sunlight, along the same path as Amadeus Klimt.

ACKNOWLEDGMENTS

I'd like to thank my editorial team of Lisa Sandell in the USA, and Barry Cunningham & Rachel Leyshon in the UK, for the time and effort they put into making this story the best it could possibly be — it's one thing to be "organic," quite another to be vague. I'd also like to thank Dave Martin for reading the script and making *his* usual incisive comments, and his son, Jonathan, whose DNA question I never did answer, but hope to get to the bottom of by the end of the series. Every author needs an expert or two, so I'm grateful to Dr. Andrew Sharp for keeping me straight on the medical issues, and the lovely Maddiemoiselle Bradshaw for correcting my schoolboy French (*très bon* or what?). Also, Maddie's mum, Terri, for finding me a book on Gustav Klimt from her school's art department. Go Radcliffe! Ed Wilson, if he had any hair to pull out, would surely have lost the lot sorting out the contracts — forget the percentages, what you need, folks, is an agent with *stamina*. And finally, I can't leave out Jay, who never quite gets the recognition she deserves — except in our house. *Wom!*

CHRIS D'LACEY

is the author of several highly acclaimed books, including the *New York Times* bestselling Last Dragon Chronicles: *The Fire Within*, *Icefire*, *Fire Star*, *The Fire Eternal*, *Dark Fire*, *Fire World*, and *The Fire Ascending*, as well as the companion *Rain & Fire*, which he cowrote with Jay d'Lacey. Additionally, he is the author of The Dragons of Wayward Crescent series. He lives in Devon, England, with his wife, where he is at work on his next book.